Featherbones

Thomas Brown

Sparkling Books

The right of Thomas Brown to be identified as the author of this work has been asserted by him in accordance with the Copyright, Designs and Patents Act 1988.

All rights reserved

© Thomas Brown 2016

This book is a work of fiction. Names, characters, businesses, organisations, places, events and incidents are either the products of the author's imagination or are used fictitiously. Any resemblance to actual persons, living or dead, events or places is entirely coincidental.

Without limiting the rights under copyright reserved above, no part of this publication may be reproduced, stored in or introduced into a retrieval system or transmitted by any form or by any means without the prior written permission of the publisher. Except in the United States of America, this publication may not be hired out, whether for a fee or otherwise, in any cover or binding other than as supplied by the publisher.

British Library Cataloguing in Publication Data. A catalogue record for this book is available from the British Library.

1.0

BIC code: FA
ISBN: 978-1-907230-51-6

Printed in the United Kingdom by Grosvenor Group (Print Services) Ltd

@SparklingBooks

Thomas Brown is a postgraduate researcher at the University of Southampton, where he is investigating the relationship between horror and the sublime in literature. He has been Co-Editor of Dark River Press, and has written for a number of magazines, websites and independent publishers.

In 2010 he won the University of Southampton's Flash Fiction Competition. In 2014 he won the annual Almond Press Short Story Competition. His first book, *LYNNWOOD*, was a finalist in the 2014 People's Book Prize. He is also a proud member of the dark fiction writing group: Pen of the Damned.

When not writing, he can usually be found waiting on his cats, or enjoying a bottle (or two) of red with friends.

By the same author

Lynnwood

Dedication

For Lucian and Andrew, still missing.

Acknowledgements

Special thanks to Aamer Hussein and Rebecca Smith, for incubating this story throughout its various drafts and for helping it to hatch.

Thanks also to Poppy Z. Brite, for saving me from the dark, and to Patty, for the introductions – and so much more. *Wormwood* forever has a place beneath my pillow.

Inspirations: Brite's 'Missing' and *Lost Souls*. Philip Hoare's *Leviathan*, and his many moving talks on Southampton. The city itself, my home away from home. Kate MccGwire and her haunting sculptures. Aronofsky's 'Black Swan'. Thomas Ligotti, Angela Carter and Clive Barker, whom I admire so much.

Thanks to Anna and the Sparkling Books team for continuing to make my writing dreams a reality.

Finally, thank you to Gill and Brian for always being there.

All my love.

Thomas Brown
June 2015
Oxfordshire, UK

@TJBrown89

"Blue, green, grey, white, or black; smooth, ruffled, or mountainous; that ocean is not silent."

H.P. Lovecraft, 'The White Ship'

Chapter One

The deep mewing of a gull draws Felix from his dreams. This close to the sea, there are many gulls. It is their city, as much as anyone else's. Pinching the sleep from the corners of his eyes, he gazes across to the window sill. The bird stands with its back to him, wings tucked to its chest, as though surveying the streets spread out nine floors beneath it. In the morning light, its feathers appear grey, and quite dirty. He makes to move from under the covers and it turns sharply, studying him with one beady eye.

For several seconds man and bird stare each other out. Then he staggers from bed and it screams at him through the glass before plummeting from the windowsill. When he realises it is Monday, he considers doing the same.

Every morning Felix walks the same way down the high street to the offices on London Road, and every evening he walks the same way home again. The sounds of the city wash over him; the murmur of car engines, gull cries, laughter as students trail past him on their way to Halls of Residence, and beneath it all the maritime roar of the sea.

His flat overlooks the docks and it takes him thirty minutes, at most, to get from one end of the city to the other. The walk is generally uneventful. He barely notices the streets any more, the pavements, the faces of passers-by. When Michael and he first took the vacancies with the recruitment agency it was a temporary set-up. He had just finished his History degree and needed money to support himself. He has worked at the agency for over five years now; five years of his life lost to the city by the sea.

The office stirs with morning activity. Years ago, the

team numbered eight. Now they are four, including Mr. Coleson. He cannot see Mr. Coleson in his office but he can hear him and his deep-bellied laughter through the door, propped open enough to remind everyone that he is there and they are here to work another week. The rest of the office is a small, communal space. The stationery drawer sits empty, functioning biros as rare as new job prospects. A cleaning rota stares back at them from the cork noticeboard on the wall, detailing precisely whose turn it is to vacuum the carpet, dust the windows, mop the lavatories, and when. No one was especially enthused when this rota was drawn up, but none less so than Maggie, who, on her thirtieth birthday, took Mr. Coleson aside and threatened to leave in a voice not unlike those belonging to the gulls outside, unless he removed her from the rota immediately. It is difficult to call what occurred that morning a conversation, as this implies there was rapport of some kind and at least two speakers. When negotiations concluded, Maggie was relegated to light dusting on Tuesdays and Fridays. She seemed satisfied by this, and Felix remembers suspecting that, for all her protesting, she was in no more of a position to leave than he.

In an ideal world, Maggie begins each day by patiently sorting through her emails, red-lacquer claws wrapped around a vast mug of tea. At her desk a strong work ethic grips her, setting her face into a mask of concentration. Blue eyes narrow. Thin lips seal tight. Loose strands of light blonde hair are dealt with swiftly where they stray across her face.

When Michael is late, however, she is forced to begin the day with his photocopying. Long talons tap the cheap plastic cover of the machine while it makes its own Monday protests beside her. Sometimes, if the photocopier is taking particularly long, she touches up her make-up in a hand mirror while she waits. Tiredness vanishes from her pale face beneath a mixture of concealer and rouge; a clown, all set for another day at the circus. He smiles to himself at the comparison, before wondering what that might make him.

Staring around him at what could be any morning of any week in the last five years of Mondays, he wonders what Maggie would do if they ran out of teabags, or if the photocopier began working properly, or what would happen if Michael was actually on time for work one day.

His friend cuts a dark silhouette as he hurries past the office window. The cold air chases after him, his black pea coat fluttering in the wind. Inside the office, he strides to Felix's desk, shrugging the coat from around his slight shoulders. Its absence reveals his white slim-fit shirt, navy blue tie, and a pair of grey trousers that Felix has long considered a touch too tight for the office. The coat flaps like a great pair of wings from around him.

"Morning," says Felix tentatively.

"My head feels like a Greek Tragedy."

Aside from the fact that he is dressed for work, the casual observer might be forgiven for thinking Michael has come straight from a bar. By the unforgiving brightness of the office lights his features seem pale, made sharp by his dark hair, scraped into a tight bun behind his head. His eyes are thin, cheeks slender, narrow nostrils quivering as they filter the scents of printer ink, carpet cleaner and stale dust that make up their surroundings.

"Have you slept yet?"

"Yes." Michael seems to reconsider. "Briefly."

"You're hopeless."

"There's always hope."

"Three years of studying philosophy and you sound like a fortune cookie."

Friday night swims behind Felix's eyes; shining spirit bottles, the shadows in the bar's rafters and the rush of the sea filling his head. He struggles to recall the face of the woman with whom Michael spent the best part of the evening, and most probably the rest of the weekend. For a moment he thinks he places her; sitting at the bar, legs crossed, a small, black dress hugging her hips, before the lights, and perhaps drink, distort her face into obscurity.

Then Mr. Coleson is standing in the doorway of his office, except instead of booming laughter the Ringmaster is tapping his watch. The gesture is empty, grown meaningless from years of repetition, but it prompts apologies from Michael and an immediate start to his working day.

The clouds break just before lunchtime. It is April, the month of showers, and Southampton's are as cold and wet as anywhere Felix knows. He spends his morning scanning profiles for suitable job applicants. It is a thankless task. The hours stretch on, during which time he wonders where he went wrong. For three glorious years he had lived the dream at university. It had given him purpose, direction, an aim. The first week he spent drunk. The second he spent recovering, from both the drink and his leg, which he injured slipping down a flight of stairs in a club. He remembers little of the first week, or the ensuing three years, all lost in a sea of liquor. He does remember feeling hopeful and happier than he has ever been, at a time when the rest of the country was struggling to make ends meet. He had even managed a degree at the end, although it hadn't been easy getting there. He owes that much to the city, at least.

And there it is. 'At the end'. There had been no afterwards, no fourth year. University had come to its champagne-popping, Graduation Ball finish and abandoned him, with nothing but a piece of paper and a false sense of hope to show for it.

After work, Felix retraces his steps through the city. The pavement is long and narrow, a pier leading first to the city centre and then the docks beyond. If he walks south through the city, or south-east, or south-west, he will come to water. There is no escaping the sea, which laps its salty tongue against the city and the people who live there.

A low wall follows one side of the pavement, barely more than knee-height, separating the street from the park grounds beyond. The stone feels cool and gravelly against the backs of his legs when he veers from the pavement to perch on it. Overhead, heavy clouds fill the bright sky, spears of sunlight struggling to pierce the swollen grey, reminding him of the hymns he used to sing when he was a boy at St. Barnaby's. Divine chariots could roll through those clouds, steeds snorting, thunder spilling from the spokes of the wheels.

"Thank God for Fridays, and men like Michael."

Opposite him there is a bus stop, behind him the green expanse of East Park. On his left a man sits cross-legged on the ground. The man's face is long, his eyes half-closed. Hands twist arthritically into the hollows of his overcoat, which is wrapped loosely around him like a second skin, ready to be sloughed. It seems impossible to accurately guess his age. From the look of his face, he might be in his forties. Felix has never seen fit to ask.

"Hello, Sam."

The man stirs slowly, seeming to come back to himself. He glances down, to a handful of change littering the pavement, then right, then up, to where Felix is sitting on the wall. His lidded eyes narrow, then flicker wide.

"Felix!"

He is not sure what first drove him to strike up conversation with Sam, when they spoke one evening last Christmas. He supposes he felt sorry for him. It was two below freezing outside and Sam made an abject sight, huddled beside the wall in the same tired coat he's wrapped in now. He offered to buy the man a hot drink, and they found a café, not far from the park, down an alley at the bottom of East Street. Sam does not like crowds, and Felix does not like what Christmas does to people. So the café became their haunt, their private place where for a short while each week they could escape the eyes and ears of the city. They have been going for coffees there together ever since.

"You'll catch your death, sitting out here. Aren't you wet?"

"I'm waiting," says Sam.

"Waiting for what?"

"The angels." Sam stares behind Felix as he speaks. "The angels are coming."

Felix follows his gaze to a statue, standing at his shoulder. In each hand she clutches a wreath. His eyes travel from her outstretched arms, past her proud face, down the flowing contours of her robes to the base on which she stands. More flowers have been placed in bouquets around her feet and he realises with a twinge of guilt that she is a memorial. Though the flowers partly obscure it, he sees a plaque, and written on it some words, partially hidden by red rose petals.

He reads the words 'Officers,' 'Duty' and 'Titanic' before a young man trips, or is pushed, and falls into the flowers. Mad laughter fills Felix's ears as the man staggers to his feet and flees the broken bouquets with his friends.

Clouds slide before the sun, turning the statue ebony, where a moment before she seemed quite green. Verdigris-copper; the colour he imagined the sea here to be, before he first saw Southampton's waters. Her austere face reflects his; flesh mirrored in forged metal.

"The rain," says Sam, smiling brightly. Black stubs glisten in his gums. "They love the rain. The water. They sing of it. I'm waiting. Beautiful voices. I'm waiting."

"Do you need to wait here? I thought we could go for a drink. My treat."

"It has been a slow day at the office…" Pinching the scattering of coins one by one from the pavement, Sam places them in his coat pocket, before turning back to the memorial. With his face upturned he could be a small boy, wide-eyed, swamped by his father's coat. "Yes, then, let's."

"You're sure?"

"Yes, yes." He breaks into a smile. "She'll wait. I could use a cup of something hot."

Felix looks up one last time at the winged silhouette, thin against the budding backdrop of East Park. A shaft of light illuminates the grey-green hollows of her face, with its tight lips, small nose and empty eyes. Then he hops from the wall, his white shirt blossoming grey with rain, and if it seems to him that the statue turns to face him as he leaves, he knows he is mistaken; a shaft of light, making movement where there can surely be none.

Hands pink from the cold clutch the wall for purchase as Sam struggles to his feet. Reaching down, Felix helps him from the pavement. The hands are much smaller than his own, and hard where they press into his palms. As they walk off together in the direction of East Street, he knows a cup of coffee cannot save those hands. Still, for an hour or two it might help keep them warm.

Chapter Two

Over the next few weeks, Felix feels drawn to the statue as he passes it by on his way into work and home again. In the mornings he has no time to stop and stare, but that does not prevent him from glancing her way as he walks through the shadow of East Park to London Road. Dawn illuminates her silhouette with its cold light, so that her slender arms appear severe, her skin sheer black and as devoid of warmth as the rest of the night-chilled city.

In the evenings she bathes in a different light, and seems the more content for it. Dusk draws a coppery green to the sculpted shallows of her face and robes, an oceanic tint dredged from the depths of the black bronze. It is during this time that she seems most radiant; an angel as he has always understood angels to be, and on more than one occasion he finds himself wondering why such statues are so often shaped like seraphim. It seems the nature of man to surround himself with Heaven, as though by doing so the world might seem more divine, or less hellish, or simply better. He sees only metal, forced into the shape of something that it is not.

When five o'clock on Friday finally arrives, the office empties. Felix remembers speaking to Michael, confirming their customary drinks, then walking home through the city. The high street stretches out before him; an endless parade of shop-fronts, multiplying in the gloom. It has stopped raining, although only recently. The ground glitters black with puddles.

At his flat, he finds leftover lasagne and a half-drunk bottle of red in the kitchen. The mince is grey, the cheese rubbery, but as the dish rotates in the microwave it slowly becomes more appetising, until the aroma of hot fat and melted béchamel makes his insides moan.

Taking himself to the balcony, he sits until the wine is gone, his stomach full, the sky a little softer at the edges. When the bottle is empty, he heads inside to get washed and changed, but not before undoing his tie and releasing it to the sky. The wind snatches the fabric, fluttering, from his hand, and does not give it back.

The walk to Ocean Village passes him by. One moment he is leaving his flat and crossing Queen's Park towards the water. The next moment, he is standing outside a bar. There are a number of bars and restaurants by the marina, each as busy as the next. Laughter spills into the cold night, which has fallen without him realising.

He follows the murmur of conversation towards the nearest of the buildings. Orange light pours from its interior into the darkness outside. One side of the bar is mostly glass doors and these are open to the night air. He makes out the languid shape of smokers, reclining in the cold, and wonders whether Michael is among them. He will be on the smoking terrace or at the bar itself.

As he enters the building he is hit by a wave of warmth and sound. Voices buzz in his ears, and laughter, and the unmistakable clink of bottles against glass. He smells cologne and wine and the freshly-chopped fruit they are slicing at the bar to put in cocktails.

"What time do you call this?" says Michael, turning as Felix approaches. He is sitting at the counter opposite two towering drinks.

"More like what do you call those?" The drinks at the bar are fiercely red, served in a fat glass brimming with fruit and ice.

"Alcohol." Grinning, Michael slides one of the drinks towards him. "Sea Breeze, I believe."

He sits beside Michael and takes a sip through one of several straws. The taste is sharp, though not unpleasant.

He relishes the sensation of the cold liquid and the warmth of the alcohol inside it.

"Sorry I'm late," he says, withdrawing his mouth from the straw.

"Your excuse, Mr. White?"

Felix shrugs. "I was eating."

"The world?"

"I was hungry," he says, smiling.

"Aren't we all," mutters Michael, scouring the crowds behind Felix. His heady aftershave fills Felix's nose. "And thirsty, from the looks of things."

"What?"

"I'd know those wine lips anywhere. You are betrayed. One glass or two? Couldn't wait to get started, I suppose?"

He realises that Michael is referring to the red wine he drank earlier that evening. "You've found me out," he says, removing the straws from his drink and taking a large mouthful. Idly, he wonders how badly his lips are stained. He hears Michael laughing, sees his face creasing up over the rim of his glass, then the drink burns down his throat and he does not hear or see anything distinctly for the rest of the night.

Michael's delight echoes across the bar. Felix hears genuine laughter, the kind that bubbles up from deep within before spilling like foam into the air. There is nothing stilted about the expressions on people's faces. Their smiles are savage, eyes sparkling, faces freed from conscious thought and consequence. All across Southampton, people are flocking to clubs and pubs to lose themselves beneath the stresses of modern life.

"Outside." Michael's breath is heavy in Felix's ear and down his neck. "Outside, I need a smoke."

They move from the bar, where Michael has been speaking with a woman, and onto to the smoking terrace overlooking the marina. As they step outside, the cold is bracing. Shivers slip down Felix's spine.

The calm takes his breath away. The blackness, too, stops him where he stands; a stretch of uninterrupted dark, which he knows to be the sea and the sky, though he cannot tell them apart. This is why they come here in the evenings, time and time again to the bar beside the sea: to drink and laugh and lose themselves in the clear breath of the ocean.

He half listens as Michael tells him about the woman at the bar. There is a name, an age, a rough score out of ten. It is a story he has heard a hundred times before. He is listening to other things: the wind, the sea, an irregular fluttering sound overhead, which he supposes is gulls, settling into the grooves of the building to roost for the remainder of the night. Gradually his eyesight grows familiar with the darkness and he makes out other details; gradients of grey spilling through the cloud-cover, tiny flashes of light like a sea of scales, where moonlight catches the waves, and small shapes in the distance, more gulls gliding silently in the night. They drink and smoke and laugh until they can do none of these things anymore and then they leave. Arm-in-arm, one silhouette against the night, they struggle into the back of a taxi.

The city streams past them, reduced to small lights, blurred lamps, an endless stretch of black that is the sky, beneath which buildings squat like old men with dour faces stationed by the sea. Felix sees his friend in flashes of illumination: strawberry stains down his white shirt, his eyes thin and wet with laughter, hair loose over his face where it has freed itself from the knot behind his head. In minutes, they are standing outside Felix's block of flats. Michael pushes a crumpled note from his back-pocket into the driver's hand. As the taxi pulls away, Felix and he stumble inside.

The brightness of the foyer burns their eyes. For what seems like forever they try to work the lift. Michael falls asleep in one corner, his face pressing against the tarnished metal walls, before Felix abandons the lift for broken. Dragging his friend to his feet, they make the long climb up the stairwell to the top floor.

When they reach his flat, Michael crawls from the corridor to the sofa and falls face down into the cushions. Felix waits until he can hear his friend snoring before taking himself to bed. He does not have to wait long. Stripping, he collapses into the coldness of the covers and closes his eyes.

His rest is fitful. More than once he wakes, entangled in his duvet, as though he has been thrashing inside it. When his bed becomes too hot, he wanders into the kitchen for a glass of water. The coolness of the rest of the flat is refreshing against his slick skin.

He fills a second glass, which he leaves for Michael, on the floor beside the sofa. His friend is facing away, curled into his knees, clutching a leather cushion like a swimming float to his chest. He has shed his shirt, and his shoulder-blades jut sharply from the whiteness of his back above the harsh track of his spine. The thought of his face, were he to wake suddenly and find Felix standing nude over him, draws quiet laughter in the dark.

A strange sense of dissonance runs through Felix, as though the sky or the city under it is shifting. The laughter dies on his lips, leaving a hollow feeling in his chest. All of a sudden he feels ludicrous, standing here naked in the moonlight beside the oblivious form of his friend. Turning, he hurries from the room.

Falling back into bed, he floats through the space between awareness and dreams. The sound of Michael's deep breaths fill his ears, echoing those of the sea outside. Another noise accompanies it; soft, like a bird crooning, and he imagines the gulls again, settling into the gutters above Ocean Village. Something slightly rotten stings his nostrils.

He has had a pleasant evening. If he is sure of nothing else, he knows this. Friday nights are always satisfying, when for a few hours each week it is possible to forget the rest of the world, drink, laugh and be content. The feeling is quite cathartic. He remembers the New Forest coven he researched for a university project; women who professed to channel the spirit of the Devil, who lived and breathed his name, while they raced naked through the trees. If it is the Devil who delights in dancing, who granted those women freedom from the strictures of their sorry lives, then he was there tonight, feet scratching out steps against the floor, tattered wings outstretched beneath his arms –

Rolling away from the wall, he turns his face to the cold side of the pillow and finds himself staring at a silhouette in the doorway.

For a few uncertain seconds he flaps like a newborn chick in his bed covers, before remembering that he is not alone in the flat. It is impossible to see Michael properly, but he makes out his friend's thinness, his slender arms, the angular profile of his face in the darkness.

"Michael?" he says, but the man is already moving away down the hallway. Sinking back into the covers, his head heavy, he wonders whether he should go after him, and with the memory of the night fresh in his mind falls into the blackness of sleep.

Chapter Three

The weekend passes Felix by beneath his bed covers, where he knows warmth and sleep, only vaguely aware of other things: a text message, the groan of the boiler, birds fidgeting outside the window. When he remembers that Michael spent the night on his sofa, he ventures from his bedroom but finds the rest of the flat empty. Standing in the main room, he looks out over the balcony. The evening and perhaps the drinks that helped make it have left him hollow and light-headed, as though he is not really in the room at all but a presence, viewing a moment in time.

During one such waking moment, he reminds himself that this is what weekends are meant for. On these days the angels themselves settle like dark sentinels in their roosts, cooing soft hymns while dreaming of life, love and whatever else might haunt an angel's sleeping thoughts. He dreams of similar things, until his alarm reminds him in its shrill way that it is Monday morning and he is due at work.

He is conscious of eating, the feel of hot water against his skin, then clothes; soft socks, stiff shoes, the tightening of a tie around his neck. As he leaves his flat, the morning breeze blows cool against his face, and while it is not warm by any stretch of the imagination, the city does not seem as cold as it has previously. This close to the coast, they are rarely without a breeze; sea-currents stripping the air of heat as they soar inland. He wonders if this is spring struggling to emerge, carried on the blossom by the same sea-salt breeze.

At the office, Maggie and Mr. Coleson are discussing the weather as though they have never seen the sun before, or felt rain against their faces. Michael appears at ten minutes past nine to find Mr. Coleson waiting for him. They re-enact their morning routine of reprimands and insincerity.

"What is it today, Michael?"

"Sorry, Mr. Coleson. Car trouble."

"I thought you caught the bus in the mornings?"

"I do. The traffic was terrible."

"We've been through this before, Michael. Rush hour traffic doesn't constitute 'car trouble'. If the traffic means you're going to keep on being late then you need to catch an earlier bus."

"Sorry, Mr. Coleson."

"You can't keep being late, day-on-day."

"It won't happen again."

Despite making good progress with his workload, Felix's day drags on. It is the affliction of Mondays, to stretch well beyond their allotted time. On several occasions, he catches himself staring blankly at his desktop monitor, lost in the infinite pattern of the pixels, or perhaps the face staring back at him. His skin is pale, his hair thinner than he remembers it being and more scant about his temples than he has cared to admit to himself before now. His eyes look different, too. They seem stonier, the skin beneath them dark and tired. It is the face of a man with a hangover; not from drinking but from living. He considers the different lives he has lived, from his childhood in proper Crows Hill, to the dark liquor dreams of university, then working life afterwards; the sort that drained the soul until he was dried up and empty.

When he tires of his reflection, Felix turns to the rain as it pours down the office windows, streaky and speckled against the glass. All of it stirs something inside him that he cannot place but feels strongly nonetheless. He was born in the rain. That night, his mother held him for the first time. Then she had died, and his father and he were alone. He had never known so much water before moving to the city, and yet he feels it is one of the things that drew him here; whether the sea, the sky or the mist that sometimes creeps across the waterfront in the mornings. Crows Hill is in Oxfordshire, far from the lick of the coast. The wettest he knew as a child was when the River Cherwell burst its banks.

***

"To the ancient Greeks, the Sirens were figures of beauty and death. If the texts agree on anything," said Mr. Stuart, "they agree on this. Half-bird, half woman, they inhabited various cliffs and islands along the Mediterranean from where they sang, and so haunting were their voices that passing sailors were helpless to ignore them, sailing to their doom, and the doom of their crews, their ships dashed to flotsam on the sharp island rocks. Classical texts are littered with their references.

"Some stories show them with the bodies of birds and the faces of women. In others, they are depicted as beautiful maidens, with talons for feet and great feathered arms. While their physical forms vary, their songs always hold the same allure. No man who heard their songs could pass their islands without being drawn to them, giving rise to the term 'siren song', which we still use today, to describe something of great appeal but ultimate self-destruction."

When the bell rang for break-time and they rushed into the playground, Harriet would sometimes run from him, or seem to hide, or surround herself with other girls so that he could not go near her for fear of attracting their laughter, their eyes.

If Harriet was his Siren then these shrieking things were the Harpies of Strophades. It was no wonder, he thought, that he had never really noticed them before. They were nothing beside Harriet, who was so different from the other girls.

"The Sirens were wild figures. Some say they devoured the flesh of those who were drawn to them, and that they sang out of hunger. Others portray them as victims of their own voices, for those who were drawn to them could never leave while the Sirens sang, and so starved to death on their island prisons, which became islands of corpses, carcasses resting amid the meadows and the flowers that grew from them.

"Whether flesh-eaters or not, it is difficult not to admire the Sirens, for they represented – like many of the Greek monsters – a force of nature, more wild and honest than anything left in the world today. They were figures of the earth and the sea and the sky, tying these things together as they bridged life and death, revulsion and beauty. Every civilisation since has created their own deathly figures; their Valkyries, Blood Eagles, Santa Muerté, but none, I dare say, as visceral and triumphant as the Sirens, who sang because they could, and flew, and feasted on life with the birds."

Harriet's whims were her own. For a week following their first meeting at the churchyard she would not sit next to Felix, nor permit him to sit beside her, when they found themselves sharing classes. He remembered hating Harriet for surrounding herself with those Harpies, then hating himself, then craving her and her voice, her company, her hand beside his. She was a wild spirit, like Mr. Stuart had said; a force of nature in Crows Hill, where everyone else was tame. For all their differences, the other girls only served to highlight Harriet. It seemed that an invisible tide emanated from her, drawing Felix closer then pushing him away. He thought it must be the way of tides, and girls, and love, though he never dared to speak such things out loud.

***

He comes back to himself slowly, drawn to the office by the tapping of fingertips on keyboards, the gradual ebb of the clock on the wall and rainfall, striking the window at a slant. In the street, a gull is scavenging from a bin beside the road. The sky, just visible over the dark rooftops, shines brightly. Tarmac seems to splash as people hurry past.

"Felix?"

Two more gulls alight in the street, then a third, and a fourth, a squabbling mass around the bin; Mr. Stuart's Sirens given feathered form, made real by the solidity of the city and the cold lash of rainfall on their backs.

"Felix?"

"Dreaming," he manages, his breath catching in his throat, while behind his ribs something shifts uncomfortably. "Daydreaming."

"Reprobate. Meanwhile the rest of us are slogging away…"

"I can see you playing Solitaire from here."

"I am not."

"You're losing."

"How dare you? I never lose!"

Drawn by the gulls' disturbance, Maggie, Michael and he assemble behind the window. The birds make a frantic sight, their wings twitching, screams filling the street. When contact is made, by a beak or broad pinion, the birds spring back from one another, as though jerked suddenly into the air like puppets on invisible strings.

It is somewhat apt that the birds draw blood here, where so many altercations reach violent heights, brought to life by the many pubs and clubs crammed into the street opposite offices, convenience stores and fast customer trade. At once an extension of the city and separate from it, an air of sullenness hangs over London Road, which is saved only by the same pubs and clubs that would see it wetted with blood; the allure of alcohol and an escape from the real world drawing the crowds of students and the homeless who, together with the birds, make up the street's cosmopolitan pulse.

"What are they doing?" says Maggie. She lingers hesitantly behind the glass.

"Fighting," says Michael.

"Why?"

"Do they need a reason?"

"Yes!"

"Food. A mate. For the sheer hell of it." Beside Felix, Michael shrugs vaguely. "They look hungry, to me."

Maggie groans audibly. "Thank you very much for that mental image."

"You do understand that birds eat bread? Flies, seeds, occasionally used chewing-gum."

"Maybe we should feed them?" The suggestion is barely out of Felix's mouth before Maggie bears down on him.

"Feed them and they'll never leave. I should know. I once fed a cat that happened to find his way into my kitchen. I only gave him scraps. Titbits, from the back of the fridge. The thing came back every morning afterwards for two weeks, trying his luck."

"Is this cat a cat," ventures Michael, "or a metaphor for a gentleman-friend you happened to pick up one night?"

At that moment one of the gulls recoils into the window. Its bulk thumps against the glass and Maggie shrieks, flinching as though struck.

"Somebody fetch a broom," says Michael, "before Maggie has a fit."

"I don't want a broom, I want a drink."

"My desk," he adds, "third drawer down."

"You keep alcohol at work?"

"Brandy, a little rum. For bird-related emergencies."

"Oh, wonderful." She relaxes visibly, before glancing back to Michael. "And he was a cat, thank you very much."

The gulls continue their chaotic dance as Mr. Coleson emerges from his office with the tired mop from the cleaning cupboard. Guttural sounds slide from the birds' beaks, then prehistoric cries as the man sets among them. The birds throw themselves into the sky, and in the flurry of feathers that follows, Mr. Coleson is stripped of his identity, broken by broad wings, white plumage. Then the birds are whisked away into the wind and Mr. Coleson reappears, red-faced, himself again.

Eventually the madness subsides. Michael makes everyone tea while Felix and Maggie sneak mouthfuls of Barbados' finest in plastic cups from the water dispenser. As he sits at his desk that afternoon, staring into the screen of his desktop monitor, Felix wonders if there is such a thing as sanity. After this afternoon, it wouldn't surprise him to learn otherwise. Giddy from rum and the break to routine, he spends the last half hour of the day suppressing laughter behind his hands.

Chapter Four

After work, Felix meets Sam at the memorial and they wander down to East Street together. The café sits near the end of a side-street. The building itself is unassuming, built of crumbling grey brick beneath an off-beige canopy. Two metal garden chairs and a table litter the front, wet with the kiss of recent rain. A half-finished drink is abandoned on the table, leftover froth spilling like sea-foam onto the saucer beneath.

Felix holds the door while Sam moves inside. If the shop front looks old, with its crumbling brick and washed-out overhang, the inside is its match; dated, archaic, "a corpse from the nineties," Sam had called it, when they first found the place. Where the competition has modernised with the turning decades, ground into sleek, gaudy coffee-producing machines, the high street equivalents of the very same espresso-makers that are their steaming hearts, this one has not. Felix understands Sam's sentiments, but he can't deny a certain charm about the place, which revels quietly in its antiquity while the rest of the city does nothing but scream.

Sam finds a seat among the dated décor while Felix approaches the counter. There are many seats to choose from. Two tiny Asian women sip at their drinks by the windows. In one corner an old man in a black raincoat seems to have fallen asleep. A solitary waitress sits behind the till, reading a slim paperback.

Service is slow. Felix can't make out what she is reading, but he assumes it is a good book. When he returns, two cups and saucers rattle in his hands. Perching on a stool opposite Sam, he slides one of the coffees towards him.

"Enjoy," he says, and means it. "I've ordered some

food, too."

"You shouldn't have…"

"It's done," says Felix.

"God bless you. He's watching over you."

"Not all the time, I hope."

"Always." Sam stops talking for long enough to inhale a mouthful of black coffee. Some of it spills from his lips, following the channels of his face to his chin.

"Steady on."

"Asbestos lips. They don't call me Thirsty for nothing!"

"People call you that?"

"A name's a name." He wipes down his face on a napkin, the tissue darkening in his hands. "We all need one."

They talk easily, as two men who have escaped the world are free to do. Mostly it is Sam who speaks. Felix doesn't mind. He enjoys listening. The waitress appears from behind the counter with two toasties on oval plates, and they busy themselves with mouthfuls of hot ham and melted cheese.

"I've been giving the shelter a second chance. Just the last few days. You know I wasn't keen on it, the first time around, but it's been cleaned up since then. I mean, as much as you could expect."

"I thought you said the shelter was dangerous?"

"There'll always be the users. But I keep out of their way. Roof's a roof, you know? At least someone up there's watching over me."

Sam drinks more, pouring coffee past his lips like it is fuel and he's been running on empty. Heat bathes the man's face, and Felix imagines it softening the leathery skin, bringing relief to the sunken cheeks. He realises it is these features that first urged him to speak to Sam, when they crossed paths beside the memorial last year. It is the face of those who struggle day to day against the world, or who have struggled with it and lost. There are so many people without friends, without family, with no meaning to their lives at all beyond the jobs they get up for each morning or the rent at the end of the month, and Sam does not even have these. So Felix talks with him, and sometimes takes him for food or a hot drink, because no one should be alone.

"Who do you have, then?" asks Sam. "I have the Lord. Who watches over you?"

"I have a friend."

"Just one?"

Harriet flashes behind his eyes, staring back at him from her unspoiled face. "Yes, just one."

"That's better than most, I reckon. I had friends, before. At least, I thought I did. But you can't have friends without a life."

"Before?"

"Before the bank came knocking. Before I was evicted. Before this." He tugs at the frayed collar of his coat, then stares off into the surface of his drink.

"You have a life, Sam."

"No, not a life that matters. Not anymore."

For a moment, it seems as though Sam is going to change the subject. He grins shakily over his china cup. The expression doesn't last.

"You'll never hate yourself more than when you wake up one morning in the doorway of a shop. You're cold. Your back aches, maybe your neck. Most mornings you can't feel your fingers. You're sitting on a doorstep under an overcast sky and you realise you're alone."

"You're not alone."

"I am. I was. No one wanted to know and I didn't want them to. I was ashamed, and angry. I wanted to break apart, to be plucked away by the angels, taken with them into the sky…"

Every evening with Sam is the same. He starts out quiet, contemplative, perhaps just numb from days and nights spent in the cold. Sometimes, Felix knows, he finds shelter, but more often than not he is stuck sleeping on the streets. As the evening progresses he grows bolder, more animated; alive with caffeine and, Felix presumes, the pleasure of companionship. Then he falls back on himself. And each time they meet, Felix promises himself it will be the last time; that he cannot bear to see Sam again, until he next sees him around town and he realises it is worse not to see him, and they go for another drink.

Eventually Sam tires, or runs out of things to say, and they make their separate ways back through the city. The streets are quiet but there are still people walking through them. There are always people. Nowhere knows the knock of shoes, the gasp of breath, the beating of the human heart like cities, which are made up of these things as much as they are collections of buildings linked by street names and labyrinthine roads. It is at once familiar to Felix and strange, so different from the town where he was born and spent the first half of his life.

He hasn't thought about home for a long time. It is peculiar that he should be remembering it now. His memories are not especially unpleasant, but he holds no fondness for the town where he grew up. Crows Hill was a conservative place, preoccupied with heritage and tradition. It still is, to the best of his knowledge. The winter floods were among the most exciting things to happen each year; wild days spent wading through the fields with Harriet.

People remember things that they love or hate. The rest smudges, as easily as the city when rain falls. Some days he cannot distinguish between the listless sea and the grey sky above it; Southampton's streets, stretching into the water, the clouds.

Chapter Five

The bar shines across the waterfront that Friday, orange and inviting in the night. As Felix approaches the building, he notices how the light catches the sea, or perhaps it is the sea that catches the light; at once dark and glassy but bright, as though burning from beneath.

Even for the weekend, the bar seems busy. Crowds have formed the length of the counter, and all of the sofas are occupied. Bodies made thin by modern life cut to the front with savage jabs from bony shoulders pressing through their clothes. Mouths grow wide when pressed to glass, desperate to drink, to speak, to scream a word or two after five days of bitten tongues and muted minds. Figures flicker in his vision; slim shapes, bent silhouettes with blemished skin and feathered arms. When Felix turns to face them, they are gone.

Pressing through the groups of people, he struggles closer to the bar. It is several minutes before he manages to find Michael, sitting patiently at the counter.

"Always early," he says, reaching over his friend's shoulder to retrieve a waiting drink. Tonight the drinks are tall and slender, filled with bright blue liquid and crushed ice. He knows Blue Lagoon when he sees it.

"Always late," replies Michael. They both drink deep from the awkward glasses, only stopping when their lips are numb with cold. "I thought you might have bailed on me this evening."

"Really?"

"Your time-keeping is terrible." He crunches on a mouthful of blue slush. "A few more minutes and your drink would've found a new home."

"I'm sure it would have," murmurs Felix, smiling. Already he can feel the alcohol heating his throat, flooding his body with warmth. The weight of the week begins lifting from his shoulders when he notices a third drink at the bar. "Didn't want to order me another, while you were at it?"

"What? Oh, that's Helen's."

"Helen?"

A slender hand finds his shoulder. It squeezes, then slides down the smooth lapel. "You must be Felix!"

For a moment it is as though the weight of the week comes crashing back down on top of him. Half-turning, he stares dumbly into the face of a woman. She smiles back at him.

"Helen, Felix," says Michael. "Are you all right?"

"Yes, sorry," he says, "the ice. Numb mouth. I just wasn't… Michael didn't mention you were joining us."

"Did too!"

"Charming," she says, smiling deeper. Moving beside Michael, she plants a kiss on his lips. "Sorry I'm late. It's horrible out there."

"Is the angel coming?" says Michael.

"Yes," she replies, looking past Felix to the crowds.

"You're sure?"

"Yes, she's coming. Angela," she says, waving, "over here."

A woman breaks from the crowd and moves towards them. As she draws nearer, Felix recognises her instantly. Matted feathers hang beneath her forearms, her bare skin pale as bone where it shines beneath the lights. Time seems to slow as he watches her advancing through the dancers, knowing – hoping – he is dreaming, and that if he is not, there is nothing he can do against this modern myth, this ancient art: the angel, resurrected by the sea, the rain, the birds in the night sky –

"Felix?"

He returns to the room and the faces in front of him.

"I… Sorry, yes." He shakes the dregs of his drink. "Drunk."

Introductions are made by the bar. Helen is twenty-six and works in retail, managing a newly-opened clothes outlet in Bedford Place. She has always lived in Southampton but would like to move to Spain when she is able, or somewhere in Italy; anywhere, in fact, warmer and drier than here. Standing by the taps in her black dress she seems familiar, and Felix feels sure he has met her before, last week or the Friday before that.

In the same breath, she tells Felix about late shifts, bank holidays, incompetent staff and a dozen other banal things that he has heard a hundred times before from as many similar faces. He nods, and smiles, and sucks loudly on his straw until she realises his glass is empty and moves away to buy a second round.

"It's heaving in here," says Michael, beside him.

"Almost too busy, tonight. A pub would be a nice change of place right about now."

"That's not such a bad idea. Next weekend."

"I think everyone has the same idea," says Angela, finishing her own drink. "Rushing out on Friday night, to drink and dance –"

"– by the sea," says Michael with her. They both look at each other and laugh easily. "You know, Angela, Felix has this theory, about the sea."

"I do?"

"You do," he says. "Remember?"

"Please, remind me."

Finishing his own drink, Michael takes their glasses and places them on the bar. "You said that this is why people come here, time and time again. Not just for the drinks but for the sea and the night sky. For the breath of the ocean on their faces."

"That's beautiful," says Angela. "Really, it is."

"Thank you."

"Do you write?"

"No. I used to, a little poetry. But not anymore."

"I didn't know that," says Michael.

"We're all full of surprises this evening."

Helen returns with a tray of cocktails and shot glasses. They drink Sex on the Beach, then more Lagoons, followed by a round of Dark 'N' Stormy, and another, until Felix cannot distinguish between the storm in his glass and the one that has broken outside, lashing the smoking terrace and stirring the sea, waves leaping like orange flames against the waterfront, illuminated and terrible by the light of the bar, where inside people drink and dance and for a few hours dream of a little life with their feet.

He doesn't remember leaving the club, or getting home, but it is still night when he wakes in his bed to a tapping sound. Slowly his eyes become accustomed to the dark. With his head on the pillow he can just make out his surroundings. The moon catches the tip of his wardrobe mirror, casting light on the skeletal frame of the clothes horse. His shirt and jeans are strewn across the floor. A flicker of white draws his eyes upwards, to where a gull has settled on his windowsill. The bird is thin, its plumage pale in the moonlight. He doesn't know how long it has been standing there, framed by the city behind it.

The tapping echoes in his head, disembodied through the darkness. The storm, at least, seems to have passed, leaving in its wake a hollow calm, like an exhaled breath. Rising, he drifts silently down the hallway. In his sleepy state he is reminded of survivors, trapped in a sunken ship, spelling out their lives in Morse Code against the metallic hull of their tomb.

For a moment he stares around, his eyesight dulled by sleep. It is still night, or early morning. He cannot remember what time he went to bed and did not think to check his bedside clock.

He examines his surroundings in the darkness. The shapes are familiar; the bookcase to his left, the drinks cabinet by the wall, the television and the plastic plant beside it. To his right he sees a pool of moonlight, captured in the clear glass table-top. The curtains are drawn but a sliver of light slips between them, near the ceiling.

The darkness alters things, so that they are not what they seem. He imagines himself in the ruins of the room, sunk deep beneath the sea, and everything around him rotten, green with growth. He is sure he has dreamed as much, before. Automatically he wades through the dark towards the curtains. Damp, maritime smells fill his nose. As his hand reaches for the fabric, he wonders what he will see. Nine floors above Queen's Park, there is no way a person has reached his balcony. He imagines one of the garden chairs being blown by the wind against the glass.

He tugs the curtains, draws them back, and finds the balcony empty.

Confusion fills his mind. He studies the balcony dumbly; the wooden railings, the table and chairs, an empty wine bottle, glass glinting in the moonlight and behind it a vast backdrop of blackness, which is the sea and the night. Both are filled with tiny stars and, he thinks, if he looks closely, a small ship, pale against the darkness. He wonders what he is doing there, standing in the cold, with only his thin cotton pyjamas for protection. Turning from the balcony, he returns to his bedroom.

The gull is still standing at the window. Behind it, Southampton shimmers in the darkness. His curtains are not drawn, accounting for the light: apartment blocks, bedroom windows and street lamps shining like the tips of deep-sea anemones in the night. He isn't sure of what time he got in, or when he left the bar, or anything beyond the room into which he has woken; the few square metres of the city that for five-hundred pounds a month he calls his own. It is at once expensive and a small price to pay for the flat that has become his home. There is nowhere else he knows like these walls, except perhaps those of the bar where he has spent the evening with Michael, and most Friday nights before that for as long as he can remember.

It occurs to him that he can still hear the tapping. He studies his room again, panning the clothes horse, the window, the wardrobe, doubting whether he is even awake and not still trapped in the throes of a dream. Then, almost helplessly he turns back to the window, and the bird standing on the sill.

Something is wrong with its face. With the cityscape behind, it is not instantly obvious, but he has the gradual impression of a gargoyle, glaring through the glass. Slowly his eyesight adjusts, the bird's features emerging from the gloom: smooth skin, fat cheeks, plump lips and two wide, unblinking eyes.

For several seconds it does nothing but stare back at him; a spectre of the city or the sea made real by the moonlight on its back. The bird shuffles, shivers, the tips of its wings tapping quietly against the glass. Then its mouth slides open and, still staring, it cries with the voice of a small child.

Chapter Six

Rain patters against Felix's bedroom window. He buries his head beneath his pillow, as though it is that easy to escape the sound, as though it is that easy to escape anything. In this half-asleep state his dream comes back to him; images rolling, crashing through his mind.

Hesitantly he wanders through his flat. As he does so he studies his surroundings: the hallway, the kitchen, the main room, as though expecting them to have changed, or for something to be waiting, behind a door or at a window. In the bathroom his reflection stares, pale-faced, back at him. On the balcony he finds a bottle where he had left it, weighing down the post. Rain has reduced the letters to sodden pulp. He wonders if he is going mad, or if he has gone mad already. It has been a long week.

"It's been a long five years," he says, as if speaking will undo the strangeness.

Opening the balcony door, he steps outside. Gull cries stretch into one sound, marrying with those of other birds. The city is made up of them. Oystercatchers potter down Woolston Beach, beaks training on insects and small crabs in the shingle. In October, Brent geese cut through the clouds like black-fletched arrows, following millennia-old migration routes from Siberia. Year out, cormorants hold court above the city, made fat and sleek on the off-cuts of those living below. He stands, their audience, while the smell of the sea fills his nose, and with it the memory of the voice from his dream; the last sound to leave Harriet's mouth, the night she drowned.

Rain had fallen for almost a week over Crows Hill when the floodgate near Burford broke. Sodden soil swept towards the town in a rippling black torrent. It spilled under the fencing that marked the Crowleys' farmstead before reaching Crows Hill Church. Statues littered the churchyard; grey figures staring skyward as the waters rushed around their robes and through the surrounding stone walls. The town was unprepared for the storm. The floodgate that kept them safe had never broken before. Not wood or stone or stained-glass window could protect them against the blackness, which poured through every gap and made gaps where there were none.

He remembers the smell, which first roused him from bed. It was a rank aroma; moist and earthy. Leaving his bedroom, he had followed the stench of soil through the house. It led him downstairs. Water met his ankles at the bottom of the stairs. He remembers lights flickering across the town. Screams followed them, and shouts, and moans that rose deep from inside people's chests; the kinds of sounds made when a person's world is washed away and they can do nothing but roar.

The Crowleys, he had later learned, had paddled through their kitchen, gathering up photograph frames and family heirlooms. Mrs. Grantham, who ran the post office in the town centre, helped drag children to safety in her first-floor quarters. Families desperately tried to repel the water from their homes, flinging it back with buckets and bowls.

He was thirteen then, too young for what had happened. He wished so hard for Harriet to come back. But there were no doctors capable of that miracle, no angels strong enough to save his friend, no God, only his dreams and his memories and horrible things that were bits of both, suffused with smells and sounds like sodden soil, slippery grass and the groan of thunder in his head; a canvas, sagging from the weight of that night, swelling, bursting, stitched back together by Dr. Moore, his mind a makeshift Shelley monster –

His weekend is lost worrying about the dream. As a boy, he had dreams often. His father called them night terrors. When he told his father that he sometimes experienced them in the day too, he arranged for Felix to see a psychiatrist, concerned for Felix's well-being in that way he was concerned for anything that might make his son different from the other boys.

"Rough weekend?" says Michael, when the pair of them slip outside for a cigarette before lunch on Monday. They are standing in an alley, by their offices on London Road. Only Michael is smoking. Felix has joined him for company and to escape the confines of his desk. He breathes in; deep lungfuls of the sea and the sky, and not a little smoke.

"Sorry, what?"

"Thank you for the phone calls on Saturday morning, too. I wasn't busy with Helen at all."

"I think I'm having dreams again."

Stiffening, Michael watches him over his cigarette. "Are you all right?"

Felix hasn't told anyone about his childhood since leaving Crows Hill except for Michael; the past made more palatable by beer and music and the intimate glow of bar light. It was enough, at university, that he was there; to study and laugh and live in a way he had not lived before. The details of his past up to that point were largely private, and his own.

He had forgotten how difficult school had been. If he sensed that he was different from the other boys and girls at St. Barnaby's, they sensed it too. He almost wished sometimes that they would strike him, that they would rise to more than name-calling, so that he might feel something, even if it was only pain. Some nights it was all he dreamed about, until he woke the next morning, dreams scattering from his head, and remembered he was alone again.

***

The boys flocked to the locker room, their cheeks red and wild from the cold. The room filled with the flutter of sleeves as they began to get changed. Socks grew long where they were pulled from toes; longer and longer until they tore from ankles, snapping like synthetic sinew through the air. It was early afternoon and the autumn wind was playing with the tree outside the window. Red leaves pressed like outstretched hands against the opaque glass.

Felix paused, his sweatshirt around his shoulders, to study the scarlet palm-prints. Their redness reminded him of other things: burst berries, split lips, the colour of his cheeks when he played outside in the cold. He stared intently for several seconds, the world around him fading beneath the brightness of the leaves. Then he lost himself once more in his sweatshirt.

Around him, the other boys pranced and preened. Sometimes their faces were expressive, wide-eyed and open-mouthed. Other times, it seemed, they barely had faces at all. One studied himself in the mirror above the sink, moving left, then right, his reflection doing likewise in the glass. From where Felix stood there was no nose, no mouth, no face that could be seen, but he imagined a sharp beak and two unblinking eyes in their place. He knew that beak. He had felt it before, or one like it, and the ceaseless peck of its words.

Shouts ricocheted from the locker room walls. When they reached the communal showers they distorted, in that way all sounds did when they bounced from bathroom tiles. He heard jubilation in those sounds, and taunts, and mimicry; so much mimicry.

The shrieks escalated, grew shrill. He stepped back to his locker, which was already open, and shielded himself behind the metal door as the boys flew into a flurry of movement. His heart rattled, a cage of frightened lovebirds in his chest.

One of the boys fell into his locker, knocking the door into Felix's face. He felt pain, where the door struck his nose. He sank to the floor. The rich metal-taste of red filled his mouth.

Blackness encroached on his vision, then whiteness, growing from the strip bulbs above. The boys circled overhead, beaks clacking, and he heard malice. He heard stupidity and joy and inconsideration. If there was an apology, he couldn't hear that. He didn't think there was.

Then they swarmed from the locker room, the corridor ringing with their shrieks. He was left alone, with the grit between his toes, the slap of scarlet at the window and the taste of the colour in his mouth.

***

"It's this world, this life," says Michael carefully. "It nurtures dreams, like a force of nature. The ones who don't dream don't stand a chance."

"Ever the philosophy student."

Michael shrugs inside his coat. He glances from his cigarette to Felix, then back again, studying the small stick between his fingers. "An ocean of wisdom, me. Life's too short to worry. Eat, drink and be merry, make every second count and all that jargon."

"Did you learn that in a lecture?"

"Second year. 'And those who were seen dancing were thought to be insane by those who could not hear the music.' Go mad, you'll probably have a better time of it."

They stand outside their offices for as long as possible. Michael cuts a convincing figure, lounging against the wall, cigarette in one hand, the other in his pocket. A mixture of admiration and envy floods through Felix. His friend makes living look effortless. He remembers the first time they met, nearly eight years ago, at the café on campus. It was a morning not unlike this one. Heavy-eyed, he had ordered a coffee from the man behind the counter. The drink looked good. He said as much. The sweet scent of syrup filled his nose, the rich roasted flavour of the bean coating his mouth and tongue.

When he looks back to that morning, he isn't sure whether they spoke or not, beyond the request for coffee. It might have been the next time, or the one following that. Turning to leave, that first morning, he had noticed the name badge, pinned to the man's polo shirt. The same was scrawled in marker-pen, down the side of the tall paper cup.

There were many coffees in the ensuing months. He became accustomed to his morning fix of caffeine and the man who made his drinks. They drank together, stronger drinks than coffee, in less reputable places filled with laughter and the thin smog of cigarette smoke. Another time they caught a train to a gig for a band they both liked. The night Michael's girlfriend, Rachel, left him, Felix was a phone call away. They walked through the city's parks for three hours, not once mentioning her name. Felix felt much better; for the man at the end of the phone and by his side in the dark.

Chapter Seven

The White Ship is at the far end of Portswood, an hour's walk from the city centre. There was a time, years ago, when not a night would go by without Felix and Michael ending up in one pub or another. Their heads foggy with drink, they would sit and talk, or else sip quietly while they melted under the twang of acoustic strings, a guitar solo or perhaps the muddy sound of a man or woman giving voice to love, life, heartbreak and other human things made honest by the breath in their lungs. Nothing sheds ghosts like good drink and a little company.

Before they leave, they linger a while on Felix's balcony. Conversation turns quickly to the evening ahead. It is a long time since they have made plans to drink midweek, but Thursday is the White Ship's live music night, and Michael had insisted. While Michael talks, Felix sips from the glass in his hand, and watches the gulls gliding overhead. He imagines they are ghosts, unfettered by the promise of a night out, released, screaming, back to the wind.

The pair leaves in good time from Felix's flat. Life is enough of a rush without having to worry about being late outside of work. Besides, Felix likes walking, or the simple companionship that comes from walking with someone, and sometimes talking.

"It's been years," says Michael as they turn from London Road. Taking a side-street, they emerge at the bottom of Bevois Valley. Michael's face seems more severe in the evening light, shadows pooling in the hollows of his cheeks and beneath his eyes. He licks his lips, hungry for the night ahead. "I hope they're as good as the last time."

"I'm surprised you can remember them after so long."

"You don't just forget a good sound. Haven't you had that? When the music stays with you beneath your skin? I just hope they haven't lost it."

This end of Portswood slumps like so much broken brick into the road. They move past shop windows plastered with newspapers, kerbs littered with soft pizza boxes and the unmistakable smell of fried food; onions, garlic, peppers and indistinct meat. They pass a Sikh temple, then a car dealership and an Aldi supermarket. Trolleys line one side of the store, and industrial waste bins, around which crowds a flock of pigeons.

"Do you remember," says Felix, as they advance towards the birds, "when we used to think they served pigeon at that place across the road?"

"We were partial to a little pigeon in the evenings."

"You were partial to a little something in the evenings."

A vague smile crosses Michael's face. "I still am."

The birds scatter as they approach. Felix feels the displaced air against his face, hears the rustle of their feathers in his ears. His world fractures beneath the buffeting of their wings. Then they are gone, replaced by twilight, tarmac and the laughter of children somewhere nearby.

The pub welcomes them with the casual ease of an old friend. It is dark inside, lit by firelight and the few dim lamps dotted around tables and the bar. They are far enough into Portswood that the student patronage does not dominate the crowd. Men and women of all sorts make up the faces in their midst. Felix sees bright eyes and rosy cheeks, coiffed hair and hair that looks like it could use a wash, vests, jumpers, the glitter of rings and gold bracelets in the firelight. In one corner, the band is setting up.

"It's good to be back," says Michael, and Felix has to agree with him. The years between now and their last visit already seem to be diminishing. Coils of knotted rope still hang from the walls, alongside framed paintings of old ships long lost at sea. And as the years shrink away, lifting from his shoulders and chest, he draws what feels like the first honest breath that week.

"Like we never left."

"You old romantic, you."

Michael moves easily through the crowds. Felix follows in his wake, comfortable for the darkness and the aroma of real ale. A model replica of HMS Grace Dieu greets them at the bar, the flagship of Henry V, where it floats inside a display case on tumultuous putty waves. They order a round from a young woman with cropped hair and a broad smile before finding a corner of the room to themselves.

The ale is rich on Felix's tongue. Each mouthful tastes fortifying, filling his arms and head with an easy fugue. Beside him, Michael is scanning the crowds. His cheeks are slightly coloured from the long walk and perhaps the hearty drink. Foam from the ale's head clings to his mouth.

"It feels strange, drinking on a Thursday. Do you still want to do something tomorrow?"

Michael finishes his mouthful before replying. The back of his hand finds his white mouth. "Tomorrow?"

"Tomorrow, as in sometime after tonight but before Saturday."

"Like what?"

"Anything. You could come to mine. Or we could do something cultural for a change. There's the Titanic museum around the corner from my place. I haven't been there for years."

"Pubs are cultural. Trust you to bring up a museum."

"I'll take that as a no."

"I would, except I've already made plans. Helen's coming over and I've promised I'll cook."

"You're cooking?"

"Apparently I'm speaking a different language here."

"Well, have you forewarned her?"

"Excuse me?" Mid-mouthful, Michael swallows quickly. "I think somewhere between telling her I can cook and trying to impress her I must have forgotten."

"Christ. What are you going to do?"

Michael stares at him a second longer, his eyes searching, before the indignation melts from his face. "I don't know. I really don't. I've been trying not to think about it."

More than once Felix notices his friend's eyes flitting back to the bar. In profile, Michael's face seems leaner. The man scrutinises the other patrons with the sharpness of a scalpel, as though by simply staring he might dissect flesh, muscle, bone and uncover the hot secrets of their hearts. He has dissected many hearts in the time they have known each other, and will doubtless dissect many more. Felix would give anything for such a gift; to be able to look at someone and see the truth of them, their carnal core.

"She's nice," says Michael quietly.

"Nice?"

"Helen. We get on. I like her."

"That's good to hear. For God's sake, make sure you cook everything through."

The first practice notes emerge from the strings in the corner. The chords reverberate in the air, sending similar

"It's good to be back," says Michael, and Felix has to agree with him. The years between now and their last visit already seem to be diminishing. Coils of knotted rope still hang from the walls, alongside framed paintings of old ships long lost at sea. And as the years shrink away, lifting from his shoulders and chest, he draws what feels like the first honest breath that week.

"Like we never left."

"You old romantic, you."

Michael moves easily through the crowds. Felix follows in his wake, comfortable for the darkness and the aroma of real ale. A model replica of HMS Grace Dieu greets them at the bar, the flagship of Henry V, where it floats inside a display case on tumultuous putty waves. They order a round from a young woman with cropped hair and a broad smile before finding a corner of the room to themselves.

The ale is rich on Felix's tongue. Each mouthful tastes fortifying, filling his arms and head with an easy fugue. Beside him, Michael is scanning the crowds. His cheeks are slightly coloured from the long walk and perhaps the hearty drink. Foam from the ale's head clings to his mouth.

"It feels strange, drinking on a Thursday. Do you still want to do something tomorrow?"

Michael finishes his mouthful before replying. The back of his hand finds his white mouth. "Tomorrow?"

"Tomorrow, as in sometime after tonight but before Saturday."

"Like what?"

"Anything. You could come to mine. Or we could do something cultural for a change. There's the Titanic museum around the corner from my place. I haven't been there for years."

"Pubs are cultural. Trust you to bring up a museum."

"I'll take that as a no."

"I would, except I've already made plans. Helen's coming over and I've promised I'll cook."

"You're cooking?"

"Apparently I'm speaking a different language here."

"Well, have you forewarned her?"

"Excuse me?" Mid-mouthful, Michael swallows quickly. "I think somewhere between telling her I can cook and trying to impress her I must have forgotten."

"Christ. What are you going to do?"

Michael stares at him a second longer, his eyes searching, before the indignation melts from his face. "I don't know. I really don't. I've been trying not to think about it."

More than once Felix notices his friend's eyes flitting back to the bar. In profile, Michael's face seems leaner. The man scrutinises the other patrons with the sharpness of a scalpel, as though by simply staring he might dissect flesh, muscle, bone and uncover the hot secrets of their hearts. He has dissected many hearts in the time they have known each other, and will doubtless dissect many more. Felix would give anything for such a gift; to be able to look at someone and see the truth of them, their carnal core.

"She's nice," says Michael quietly.

"Nice?"

"Helen. We get on. I like her."

"That's good to hear. For God's sake, make sure you cook everything through."

The first practice notes emerge from the strings in the corner. The chords reverberate in the air, sending similar ripples through the crowds. Some people return to their seats. Most show no outward sign of hearing the sound at all, content to mingle, make conversation with their friends and family; whoever constitutes their company this evening, standing beside them in the shadows, by the bar or near the log fire.

"You really don't remember them, do you?"

At the sound of Michael's voice, he turns back to the table. Michael is watching him over his pint.

"Remember who?"

"The band."

"Should I?"

"December of our first year. We caught a train to Manchester. It was cold. The carriage was filthy. There was a woman with the drinks trolley. A pretty thing, really, looking back. Big eyes, foxy face –"

"She obviously made an impression."

Michael stares at him a second longer, then turns his eyes to the firelight. Felix can see the flames dancing in his whites.

"Outside was dark from about four o'clock. We were the only two in the carriage. It reminded me of the Tube, back home, going from borough to borough to see friends, eat out, hit pubs. I always hated the Underground."

"We were drunk on those cheap Polish beers."

"Yes! Too drunk for trains. We plugged in to my mp3, an earpiece each, stuck some music on to pass the time. You fell asleep almost straight away, but I made it through the whole album."

Realisation dawns on Felix, and when he turns back to the band he sees them with new eyes, or old eyes that remember what has been. They looked different back then, of course. They have aged. But it is them.

"Featherbones," he breathes. "We followed them up there."

"They were playing in the city, just for December. We used up the last of our student loan getting there and back. The next night we watched them play live. A pub, just like this one. I suppose they're all the same, really, when it comes down to it. It was a good weekend."

"I'd forgotten. The band, I mean. The sound." He struggles for the right word to express himself. It isn't just the band he had forgotten, or their particular music, but the way they made him feel and what they stood for.

"I thought hearing them again might help to take your mind off things."

"I think you can take credit for that."

In the corner, a man steps up to the microphone and begins to sing. His voice is sensitive but strong, its softness complementing the confident tone. It washes over Felix and through him, seeming to ache behind his ribs. Around him the shadows melt in the firelight. Darkness runs like oil from the four corners of the room, inside which people swim; pale arms, slender legs, white faces filled with whiter smiles behind which shine the black hollows of mouths wide with simple pleasure.

For almost a minute the man sings alone before the assembly, although it seems much longer to Felix. Then he is joined by a guitar and the voice of the woman on his right, and the sharp cry of a violin, played by an older man with closed eyes and a slight smile. They sing and play together, making music that melts the dark, stoking the flames in hearth and hearts until the room seems to burn; a conflagration of good times relived, revived by two friends with laughter on their lips.

When the set finishes at closing time, Felix and Michael are among the last to leave the pub. The walk back into the city is long. They find themselves wandering the streets, but the night is not so quick to leave them behind. Shadows flutter in the corners of Felix's eyes. Michael's laughter fills his ears, mingling with memories of the music, still audible in the quiet. They seem to glide through the cold air.

"Come on, you!"

"Hurry up!"

"Time waits for no man!"

He follows Michael as far as the Itchen Bridge before abandoning his friend in favour of bed. He is exhausted and Michael is not far from his own house. As Felix walks away from the bridge, he feels something inside him other than laughter or the music that still plays back in his head; about eight pints sloshing in his stomach. He waits until Michael is out of sight before rushing to the side of the bridge. Rough sounds of sickness echo in the night. He tastes bitter blackness, and relief.

The river beneath him is a ragged thing. It shivers and crashes against the urban sprawl, for no reason in particular save that it is a river, and that is what it does. He remembers another river, no less temperamental. Most years it barely reached its banks, except once, the night he was born screaming into the rain, and again, when it returned to take his friend.

***

"The Romans," said Mr. Stuart, from the front of the classroom, "called the river 'tamesis', adopted from its old Celtic name, which was 'tamesas', or 'dark'."

"Dark, sir?"

"An apt name, don't you think?" he said, moving to

change a slide on the overhead projector. The light from the machine threw a long silhouette against the screen behind him. The room wavered with shadows.

"Rivers aren't dark, sir."

"They're blue."

"No, they're green! I've looked myself!"

"Yes, George, yes!" said Mr. Stuart, gesticulating widely. "They are green and blue and a hundred other hues besides. We know about light and refraction and the transparent properties of water nowadays but to the Romans it was a mysterious thing. Water was life and death. They revered it and washed in it and worshipped it as a god, a secret-keeper, a source of worldly truth. I think," he said, his glasses flashing as they caught the light, "we can call the river dark."

***

When he is sure his stomach is empty, he makes the rest of the way home through the streets. He should be feeling content, happy, exalted even. Instead he feels strangely hollow, as though at any moment he could throw himself from the bridge and be with the clouds in the night sky. He doubts he will be able to recall much of the evening in the morning but that doesn't seem to matter. In this moment, nothing matters. His blood singing, he wanders through the night.

Chapter Eight

A new day struggles to dawn through the hazy fugue that inevitably follows a night spent celebrating life. Felix imagines himself sitting statue-like at his office desk while Friday speeds around him. Maggie's crimson nails turn her hands into blurs of bloodied fists at her keyboard. When she flits back and forth between her files and the photocopier, she becomes a vague, ghostly shape. The antique machine flickers with near constant use like a strobe light in the corner of the room.

Outside, London Road is much the same. Bodies whir past the window, pulled by an invisible current, except for one figure, stationary outside the office window. Rain reduces the onlooker to a streaky silhouette. Felix's first thought is that it is Michael, recognisable by his lean shape and long black coat, except he knows that is not right. His friend is still sitting hunched at his desk, where Mr. Coleson left him that morning. Perhaps it is Sam, come to find him at work, or another of the many homeless who wander London Road. His arm moves slowly from his coat to his side, and Felix realises he is feeding the birds.

He glances away, and when he turns back to the window there is only the silver sky, the dark street and the stark whiteness of the swarming birds. The sky flashes where clouds occasionally slide before the sun. Shadows spill like ink stains across the road before seeming to vanish like so much water down the drains. Sitting in the easy suspension of his swivel-chair, Felix wonders when it was that everything started to slip away.

Once there had been a clear distinction between dreams and reality. Physically he was bound to Crows

Hill, but dreams offered him something else; a place where he could run and shout and fly. Even when they turned to Harriet, slipping into the dark, swallowed by the black flood waters, it was all right because she had meant a lot to him and he was 'dealing with her death'. Dreams, he learned, were not always happy things, but they were honest, and he would rather be upset and alive than indifferent, and not care at all.

The rain stops just before lunch time. Felix and Michael buy sandwiches from the supermarket and eat together on the wall beside East Park. The wall is wet; the park behind reduced to glistening undergrowth filled with slick leaves and trees crocheted with bright cobwebs. Michael's coat keeps the worst of the damp from their trousers.

They eat in comfortable silence. The street is surprisingly peaceful for a Friday, footfall no doubt driven away by the turn in the weather. Still, Felix finds it difficult to relax. Normally he would cherish rare moments such as this; the city softened, quiet, shining with water and light. Even the traffic seems regulated, as buses make their rounds at the stop across the road. Shivering inside his shirt, he casts a quick eye over his shoulder. Pigeons wander under the trees, and at the feet of the memorial statue. Otherwise, the park is empty.

It is easy to think that he has only recently started dreaming again; that something here, now, has begun opening his eyes. He sees the city more clearly than he has ever seen it before, and yet it is also murkier, as though the sharpness of his clarity is cutting into the streets, opening wounds that bleed like black clouds of sediment in the sea.

There were many dreams when Harriet drowned. He cannot remember them all but he remembers the pain, as though he too had drowned that night, and continued to drown ever since, sinking deeper and deeper beneath the black surface of the world, where everything is dark and muted, and he is alone.

When he gets home from work, he heats some dinner in the oven and tidies the flat. Depositing half of the ready meal onto a plate, he takes himself onto the balcony to eat. Steam pours from the pile of hot food into the cold air. Like the waves below him, he shivers. Still, he lingers outside, where he feels the teeth of the wind and the screams of the birds that it carries.

After dinner, a part of him wants nothing more than to curl up in bed, safe beneath his covers, and sleep. He contemplates calling Michael, before deciding that's out of the question. Helen will have arrived by now. The two of them might be eating. More likely she is filling up on wine while Michael wrestles with their main course in the kitchen. Felix imagines dimmed lights, dark eyes and the floral scent of a sweet white, underneath which blooms the acrid tang of burning from the next room. Throwing on a jacket, Felix ventures into the city.

He doesn't think about where he's going. There is no direction to his mind, let alone his feet, so he is unsurprised when they retrace the walk they make to work and back each day. He makes it as far as East Park before veering from the street. Sam is sprawled out beneath the memorial. He looks up as Felix approaches, breaking into an eager smile.

"Felix."

"I thought I might find you here."

Sam stares back at the memorial. "I'm still waiting."

"Fancy a coffee? I could use a pick-me-up."

He doesn't need to ask Sam twice. Gathering his loose

coat about himself, the man struggles to his feet and they walk briskly in the direction of the café. They are sitting across from each other over their drinks before Felix begins to feel more like himself again. This late into the evening, they are alone. He clutches the cup close while blowing gently on the surface. The heat from the coffee warms his hands. "Still swimming?"

Sam mirrors Felix's pose around the drink. "Swimming?"

"Keeping your head above the water."

"Oh, yes. Quite the swimmer, me."

The waitress appears with a bacon roll, announced by the aroma of hot fat and a kitchen timer from somewhere behind the counter. Sam eats slowly but with obvious pleasure, savouring the meal with his eyes as much as his mouth.

"I looked for you earlier."

"I was up by Itchen this morning." Sam tugs a napkin from a dispenser on the table beside theirs, wiping carefully around his lips before continuing. "Then the service, at Holy Waters, when it started to rain."

"What's Holy Waters?"

"The church, over by Old Town. I go there quite a lot, nowadays. Stopped by once, last winter. I only went inside to keep warm but I got talking with the vicar. A couple of others go too. I was never much of a church-goer before, but they're a good bunch."

"That's good, Sam. Really."

"It is. There's a spread sometimes, and the vicar tells us about Jesus Christ and the angels. He says we're his flock."

"Of birds?"

The man shakes with quiet laughter, his face vanishing

behind his small hands. "I mean His flock. He looks after us when it gets too much. It does get too much sometimes."

His laughter trails off but his hands do not move from his face. They sit like this for several minutes while an indifferent dusk fades across a city stirring with artificial light. In the alley outside the café, a deluge of shadows floods the wall, then drains away beneath glow of street lamps, scattering headlights and the light from wakening apartment blocks. Eventually Sam's hands return to his saucer. His fingers, at least, do not look as pale as when they left the park.

"He sounds like a good man, this vicar. Everyone needs someone like that."

"You know, I never used to think so. Not before. I didn't need any of that back then. Who goes in for God when you're on top? But now it's different."

"How?"

"He helps. It helps, to have someone to talk to, to listen."

"We're talking, aren't we?"

"Yes! But sometimes I have questions that I can't ask out loud. If you say something out loud, then that makes it real, doesn't it?"

"I think so."

"Well, He knows everything already. He's always listening. I don't go in for any of the biblical talk, except for what the vicar sometimes asks us to read, but it helps to know He's there. Him and His angels, beside me in the cold and in the rain."

It is a pleasant notion. Felix can't deny the appeal of an all-knowing, all-loving God, the belief that He is nearby, watching, caring. But he can't buy into it. When Harriet drowned, He was not there. She died in His garden, surrounded by the angels, and they did nothing. He did nothing. Either He is not there, and they are alone, or worse still He does not care at all. Felix sips at his coffee, and studies its sheer black surface, and says nothing.

Sam seems different this evening. When their cups are empty they order a second drink, but the caffeine doesn't touch him. He remains calm, clear-eyed, as though he has resigned himself to something that has been weighing over him, and is at peace.

When they are full of coffee they walk back together to East Park. Like a painting left too long in the rain, the city grows sodden, seeming to melt around them. Streets spill into the pavements that once marked them, forming endless rivers of dark grey. Buildings blur beneath the skyline, which seems to sag, then sinks beneath the sheer weight of water pressing down on it.

Walking past rows of shop-fronts, Felix sees the mobile phone stand; its devices crawling with long crustacean limbs. In the windows of clothes shops, mannequins flounder desperately behind the glass. Plastic fingers press against their prison as they drown in retail depths, heads turning to follow Felix as he passes. Even gaudy banners appear distorted, drained of their colour, like a soluble dye, bleeding into a wash, or a fresh wound under water. He keeps walking until they reach the park.

"Will you be okay from here?"

Sam is not listening, staring instead into the darkness over Felix's shoulder. Half-turning, Felix follows his gaze. East Park stares back at him, a stretch of blackness that is trees and bushes and the memorial.

The angel does not look quite the same in the darkness. She seems smaller than he remembers, thinner.

He cannot make out her face but he feels her eyes on him, staring with the blind intensity of statues. Her skin is black in the moonlight but weathered, warped by the very city that has done the same to him. Her pride seems diminished, defiance drowned beneath the anonymity of night and he wonders if this is her natural state now; if all things wither and die when they are forgotten by the world. A gull has settled on one outstretched arm. The vastness of the white bird looks obscene against her slender elegance.

"Thank you," says Sam suddenly.

"What for?"

"For listening. There's not many who listen, who notice me. If they do, it's to cross the street, or look the other way as they walk past."

"Of course. Are you all right?"

The breeze rushes through the park behind them. Felix can hear it against the leaves, sighing like invisible surf as it breaks against branches and trees. The sounds of the city well back in its wake but they are muffled, made distant as though he is hearing them through water. A car pulls past, followed by the frantic flutter of wings. He turns back to the park but can see nothing except the trees.

"I think you know, Felix. I think you know what it feels like, maybe, to be invisible. People avoid anyone who's different, like it's catching, as though by speaking to the sick or the weak they might grow weak or sick too."

"I'm not different."

Fingers that have not known proper warmth for a long time reach out, closing around Felix's wrist. They tremble wildly. "I'm all right. I just needed to say thank you."

"What's brought this on, Sam?"

"They love the rain. The water. They sing of it. I'm waiting. Beautiful voices. I'm waiting."

"You're not making sense."

Releasing his hold on Felix's wrist, Sam sinks his knees by the road. He throws his open palms into the air in a parody of worship, and Felix notices for the first time how black they are, how truly filthy he is. "I've waited," he says, "I've waited with you. Let me sing. Please, let me fly. Let me live!"

It occurs to Felix that Sam is no longer speaking to him. When Sam does not stop trembling, Felix walks forward and holds him. Unable to look down at the man by his feet, he stands stiffly, and bites his lip, and stares skyward. From its perch on the angel's arm, the gull turns and stares down at him with the same child's face Felix saw at his window. Incapable of moving, he clings to Sam, while the child's small mouth opens and it cries for them under the vast starry sky.

The initial awkwardness of their embrace gradually lessens. Discomfort slides into something else, almost a quiet relief, and only when he hears other people approaching do they break suddenly apart, and he realises just how tightly he had been grasping the man at his waist.

Sam sinks from his knees to the pavement. Felix remains with him for the best part of the night, propped up against the low wall while the shadows ebb around them. Occasionally a car speeds past, more often than not a taxi, appearing as though from the darkness as it ferries men and women through the city. Those who do not see fit to need a lift stagger down the road in their twos and threes, laughing as the night-time tide pulls them along, first towards the city centre, then, later on, home again. Eventually even they diminish.

He can't have closed his eyes for more than a few seconds, yet when he opens them again, Sam is gone. Nothing around him stirs; not East Park, not the distant high street, not even the black sky. In this moment, he might be utterly alone in the city, except for the angel, standing behind him at her plinth, and the fat gull on her arm.

Chapter Nine

Felix can't remember the last time he walked the city so early on a Sunday. He doubts he has done so since his student days; when he approached the morning from the other side, the night beforehand. Sitting outside the Church of Holy Waters, he waits for the service to finish. He resists the urge to check his watch, as he resists most urges these days, choosing instead to perch patiently on a bench, across the road from the building where the angels make their righteous roosts.

If it is a long time since he was last awake this early on a Sunday, it is longer still since he has been to church. Not since leaving Crows Hill has he walked between the pews, or held a hymn sheet in his hand. Even before Harriet's death, church was never for him. He hadn't known that as a boy, of course. His father was a devout traditionalist, if not a devout Christian, and his father's word was law in Crows Hill, where the skies were blue, the buildings old and nothing ever changed.

It took the parish many months to correct the terrible damage wrought to their church by the flood waters, thirteen years ago. The church took the longest to repair for funds had to be raised and heritage recreated, although there was no lack of generous sponsorship from the townsfolk, who wanted only for routine to return and things to become as they once were again. Felix remembers the ruin, as he remembered it whenever he had wandered the churchyard after the service. The stained glass was amongst the most costly of the work, where branches and furniture had swept through the centuries-old designs, seconded only by the statues in the churchyard, which needed returning to their pedestals. As the waters had slowly drained, the missing angels emerged in various places across town, no doubt dragged there by the flood waters, their smiling faces black with soil and slime.

When Sunday Service ends and the church empties, he enters Holy Waters. Walking quickly through the foyer, where several people are still talking among each other, he moves into the body of the church. As he passes through the doors, he slows, coming to a standstill.

The room is vast, seeming more so for its emptiness. Figures decorate the ceiling in beautiful intricacy; depictions from The Book of Sin brought to life in vivid brush-stroke. Stern-faced men smite the Sinful Courts to the corner of the masterpiece, where they cower in darkness and shadow. Reverence hangs in the air; thick, like incense or a guilty conscience, and dust coats the armaments, visible as tiny motes on the light through the stained-glass windows. More depictions of Sin dance in the windows, monstrous stained-glass images, bright and bloody with colour. They seem to snarl with incandescence as he enters.

The light, the colour, the dark, dusty shadows weigh down on him as he advances down the aisle. He walks quickly, looking neither left nor right, and is relieved when he finally reaches the front. He can't remember what they used to call this part of the church. It has been too long since he last recalled such terminology. He does remember the altar, though; a dominant presence at the head of the church, and the pulpit to the side, from where God's voice might be heard again, if he only listens hard enough, and perhaps other voices too, singing to him through the ages, though they could just belong to the wind, screaming outside.

***

Tall figures towered over Felix; the black-uniformed shapes of the grown-ups, and above them the hallowed heights of Crows Hill's church. He had never studied the rafters before, or wandered through the pews as he did now. His father guided him to a seat. The wooden benches felt hard against his thirteen-year-old skin, and smelled of strong polish, like the sort he had been taught to use on his shoes.

Crossing his hands over his chest, he stared down at his smartly-pressed trousers and his black suit-jacket. The jacket felt smooth against his hands, and he grasped it tightly, as though anchoring himself to here, to now. He had dressed smartly lots of times before. His father hardly let him out the house without ensuring he looked his best. But this time it felt different.

Harriet wouldn't have cared if he was dressed-up or not. She was dirty knees and muddy hair and blades of grass stuck to her shoes. She was running down the corridor and climbing trees and laughing so hard your voice carried right through the churchyard and you fell over with tears in your eyes. This wasn't her; rows of people, sitting, sobbing, buttoned-up, faces down.

Slowly the pews filled with people, until he was surrounded by a sea of black clothing. Music played from near the pulpit; a weak, tinny sound. He recognised the song as one of Harriet's favourites, as though she could hear it now, as though she could hear anything anymore. Perhaps that is why they played the music here. Perhaps this wasn't for God but for Harriet and the others, so many others who had gone before her over the years, over the world, more than he had ever considered before, alive then gone with nothing to show for themselves but a headstone and no guarantee of anything beyond death but that which the angels promised, the same angels who presided over the churchyard, watching the procession from the alcoves.

A friend or relative behind Felix still sobbed, but most of the assembly was silent. His father was sitting beside him, but he didn't turn, didn't look; didn't want his father to see the tears running down his face. He reached out instead, feeling the smooth wood of the bench, the dry paper of a hymn sheet.

He wanted to tell them about the morning in choir practice, when Matthew Petty had stolen his hymn sheet, and Harriet and he had spoken for the first time. He wanted to read the poem that Dr. Moore had persuaded him to write. He wanted to talk about his Classics class, where he realised how beautiful Harriet was, and how much she meant to him. More than anything he wanted to tell them about the graveyard, not ten metres from where they were sitting; about running in the rain and laughing and chasing Harriet between the headstones, beneath the smiling faces of the angels.

Felix's fingers clenched his jacket. Heat pressed against his chest and down his arms, which he realised were shaking. He wished he could shout, as loud as his lungs would let him, over and over until he couldn't breathe to speak, and run, and cry until all he could do was laugh. Instead he was forced to sit, as still as the statues in the alcoves, and be silent. The vicar's words faded out of meaning, and Crows Hill with them. Everything around Felix grew grey and mute, so that only he was left behind.

Harriet's parents were the next to speak, standing together before the congregation. Felix had not seen her parents properly before, and was surprised at how much she had looked like her mother.

Mr. Green didn't speak for very long. When he did try

to talk, his voice was thick and broken. Beside him, Harriet's mother looked thin and drawn-out, but when she spoke she remained strong, and Felix found himself remembering Harriet; the way she floated face down in the water, the way her arms and legs spread out, like she was seeing into the depths, noticing them, as she had noticed so much in life. He remembered the coldness of the rain against his skin, the blackness of the sky and the water, the statues, their faces flashing, smiling in the lightning, then mouths wide, screaming, others missing from their stands, taken to the waters, the clouds, in celebration of the savagery, the storm-tossed skies –

Mrs. Green said everything that her husband had been unable to, and it was not long before the room filled with the sound of upset. The coffin was carried away and everyone followed after it, everyone except Felix, who stayed at the front, and his father, standing beside him.

Chapter Ten

Felix doesn't remember leaving the Church of Holy Waters, or retracing his steps through the streets. He does remember the overcast sky outside; darkness that seemed to spill into the city below, diluting everything with shades of grey and shadow. He remembers the lightning, illuminating the church's crumbling walls, the Sins that seemed to watch him, grinning monstrously in the window glass, and the sound of the city, like he has never heard it before. There were no distinct noises of their own, only an orchestra of chaos, at once screams and shouts and the roar of traffic and the sea, crashing inside his head: this, God's earth, a chorus of cries.

At his flat, he finds wine in the refrigerator. Returning to his post on the balcony, he takes a swig, swilling the liquid around his mouth, allowing it to coat his tongue and teeth. Pouring the rest of the wine into a glass, he places the empty bottle on the table.

For several minutes he does nothing but sits and stares out over the sea. His flat overlooks one of the city's various dock gates, where cruise ships come to spew their living cargo onto land. There are no cruise ships today. There is only Felix and the birds that have been haunting his thoughts.

The cries of the gulls ring in his ears, reminding him of Odysseus, Tiresias, Witch-Circe and the Sirens. How long ago school seems now, how uninteresting it seemed then. He had hated learning, confined to desks and chairs. Still, the knowledge learned there seems to have stuck, or if not knowledge then awareness, inspired by those epics.

***

They studied classics with Mr. Stuart in the corridor down the east wing. Felix's twelve-year-old mind did not think schools should have wings. They were the make-up of birds and Sirens and Harriet Green, who was arguably both. From the light of the overhead projector, he traced the myriad particles of dust, which floated on the air like silt in muddied waters. The weight of the classroom washed over him like those same waters, stifling his breath until he thought he might never taste fresh air again. This was his lasting impression of his time at school, through which he was dragged, year by year, like a pebble across the riverbed.

Harriet excited him in ways he had never before known, or been able to relate, until he learned one day of Odysseus and the Sirens. Where the other girls were beginning to fill out, Harriet had a slender, almost boyish figure. Felix did not know many details surrounding this, except that she was beautiful.

"Tell me, Felix," said Mr. Stuart, "tell me what the Sirens were."

The classroom in which they sat was dark and stank of decay. Mr. Stuart had been using the overhead projector again – one of his favourite teaching tools – and the smell of burned dust hovered on the air. The smell infused the corridor, the whole school even; an ancient preparatory establishment, built on traditions no less ancient or preparatory.

"Odysseus encountered them on his Odyssey, sir."

"Yes, that much is given, Felix. But what actually were they?"

He did not know the answer because he hadn't finished his prep. Instead he had gone with Harriet to the churchyard near the Crowleys' farm. Mr. Stuart seemed to feel he was better than Felix because he was grown-up and well-educated but he had never loved anyone like Felix loved Harriet. Even Felix's father had loved his mother. Mr. Stuart was alone in the world, so could not comprehend Felix's feelings for the girl sitting in the chair beside his.

When Felix first spoke to Harriet, before hymn practice one Sunday morning, she offered to share her verse sheet with him. The hall was vast, and uneasy with the stressed sounds of old wood. Winged statues watched them from the alcoves. On that day he noticed none of this, only the quickness of his breath, the quiet of the hall, the closeness of the girl on his right.

"Hello," she said.

"Hello."

"Matthew Petty's taken your hymn sheet. I saw him do it, the little pest. Would you like to share?"

He told her he would. He had never stood so close to Harriet before. She had a peculiar smell that he couldn't then identify, but was dull and faintly earthy. Her hand, which grasped one side of the hymn sheet, was smooth and delicate-looking. He thought his own looked pale beside hers, and sought to hide most of it behind the paper.

Then she had sung. Oh, how she had sung! He did not look her in the eyes for the entire practice, but thanked her afterwards before running off to the playground, red-cheeked and breathless, after the other boys.

***

He stands listening to the gulls until his clothes are soaked, his skin cold; wet with rain. Their screams are wild and he understands Odysseus' angst, or that of the Sirens. In that moment he wants to write of the gulls, to sing of them, to dance through the skies with them, except he can do none of these things very well. He imagines he is winged and among them; the wind in his feathers, cold rain and screams on his lips.

He contemplates throwing his phone over the balcony. The ground is nine floors below, and the phone would be obliterated. He pictures the moment of impact in slow-motion; the thin, black case as it cracks against the pavement, the sound of destruction, short and immediate as a breaking egg, or life itself, shattering into a hundred shards against the unforgiving ground.

His hand slips into his pocket. For a moment temptation spurs him to hold the mobile over the railings, arm outstretched; as supplicant as the statue in East Park.

The silver skies match the silver seas, which shudder underneath, the tips of their waves shivering and white. Withdrawing his outstretched arm from the railing, he studies his hands. They are the same hands that held Harriet's, and they are not. Now they hold wine bottles, and sometimes a desktop mouse, and not much else. The life he has lived is legible in their creases; a callus here, where he has worn down his skin, a wrinkle there, when another year slipped past him. The fingers of his free hand grip the railing of the balcony. The wood is wet but flaky, where rainfall has worn through the polish. He rubs the railing so that a little more crumbles free. It is carried off by the wind, and some of Felix with it.

He realises he is still holding his phone. With numb fingers he files through his contacts. It is not a long list. It has never been a long list.

"Michael?"

"Hello, trouble. To what do I owe this honour?"

"You said it would be all right."

"You didn't... Felix?"

"It's not all right. I need to talk to someone."

"Yes, of course. Are you at home?"

"Yes."

"Wait there for me. Just wait."

The gulls are still screaming. He fancies they are speaking to him. "The angels," they scream, "the angels are coming. Jump, Felix. Jump from the balcony and fly with us." A deep, singular terror tightens his chest, not at the prospect of plummeting, but that the thought had crossed his mind at all. Then he prefers that the birds are not speaking, incapable of such a complex thing, content to scream into the wind.

Chapter Eleven

Felix is still sitting, shivering, on the balcony when Michael finds him. It seems only seconds since they spoke on the phone. They go inside together, and he changes into a dry set of clothes while Michael makes them both a drink. He isn't sure whether drinking is a good idea or not, but he takes the glass anyway. Michael is only trying to help.

He knows he is warm again, and dry, because the glass feels cold in his hand. It is black with cola, and smells of rum. The first sip makes him wince. So does the second. By the third sip, he is not thinking about the taste, or anything at all except the night Harriet drowned. He takes a seat beside Michael on the sofa.

"Come on, then," says Michael, lifting his glass to his lips, "what's brought this on?"

"I went to church."

Michael splutters into his drink. "Well, that would do it."

"I thought it might help."

"I'm not sure it's working."

He tells Michael about Crows Hill, and how his memories of the town have been coming back to him. He tells him about all the moments that are surfacing in his head and floating there, like the bubbles in their drinks. He tells him about the pain inside, and how he thought he had escaped it when he escaped Crows Hill, but that it is still there, and has been all along, growing inside him.

"I'm seeing things," he says, as they are finishing their drinks. His tongue feels thick, mouth sticky with a coating of cola. "The angel, from the memorial at East Park. And Harriet. Her face."

"Seeing things?"

"Dreaming, I suppose. But I'm awake."

For a long moment, Michael is silent. Gull song fills the void; long, lilting sounds from outside the balcony. Felix watches his friend, who is studying the shining black surface of his drink, and wonders what his eyes see there, bobbing in the blackness.

"What was she like?"

"She was brave. Wild. Careless, in that way some children are."

"No, what was she like?"

"I think she was lonely."

Putting his drink to one side by his feet, Michael swoops forward. He grasps Felix by the thigh. His fingers are firm where they latch onto him. His breath is sugary and cold.

"Eight years and counting. A lot of this is new to me, but I know you. I know you enjoy the job about as much as I do. I know five years is too long to be sitting at a desk. You expected more from life. I know because I expected more too. And we'll find it. We will. In the meantime, we need to keep going. That's all anyone can do. Yes?"

"Yes."

"Remember what you said before, about the bar? You said 'This is why people come here, time and time again. Not just for the drinks but for the sea and the night sky.'"

"'For the breath of the ocean on their faces.' You remembered."

"Of course I remembered. Hold on to that, Felix. If it's the only way to keep your head above the water, hold on to it. I know I will."

"How's Helen?" he says absent-mindedly. Staring at

his hands, he senses Michael smiling.

"She's good," he replies. "Angela's good too."

Releasing his grip, Michael leans back into the sofa. They both take a mouthful of their drinks. The wind breathes heavily against the glass balcony doors.

"How long has it been?" says Michael suddenly.

Felix doesn't need to ask to know what he is talking about. "Two years," he admits.

"Two years! No wonder you're feeling pent up. Don't you miss it?"

"Are we really going to have this conversation now?"

Michael shrugs. "Now's as good a time as any."

He thinks about what he is missing, about the stream of women Michael professes to sleep with; a production line of faceless bodies, shining with sweat, grasping for attention, affection, connection in a world that requires it but provides none. He thinks about the phone calls, the arguments, the birthdays and forgotten anniversaries that seem to constitute Michael's non-working life; his colleague, Lothario, living the dream-life in Southampton city centre.

"No," he says. "Yes and no. It's complicated."

"It's not really, though, is it?"

Shaking his head, he watches the last of Michael's drink as it vanishes down his throat and wonders whether Helen really knows what Michael is like. He wonders if Michael himself knows, and if Helen would care. Mostly he wonders how Michael lives with himself day after day, and it is then that he realises why man surrounds himself with angels. It is not because the angel reminds him of Heaven or death but because she is a woman.

An angel is a messenger of God, but a woman is His

child and so much more; a mother, a daughter, a sister, an instinctively maternal being. And as much as man needs reminders of Heaven and death, he also needs woman, whichever role she might play, to keep him safe, to keep him sane, to keep him singing in the night, until his song is spent.

It is almost dusk when Felix and Michael find themselves in East Park. The idea was Michael's, inspired sometime around the last half-inch of the rum. The city is shrouded with dusk. Still, its sounds wash over them; the roar of traffic, the rattle of construction, voices as people flock past them through the park on their way back to wherever they call home.

When they reach the memorial, Michael and he perch on the low wall. Huddled into his hoody, hands firmly stuffed into his pockets, Felix turns on his seat and peers up at the statue. She stares stonily overhead.

"We've stopped by here before, you know." As he speaks, Michael produces a pack of cigarettes from his pocket. He proceeds to light up. "The night Rachel left me. We must have lapped East Park a dozen times. It looks different in the dark. I've never really noticed."

"Noticed what?"

"The memorial. The little details. I suppose I've never really looked."

They sit staring at the statue, surrounded by the city-roar of traffic, the hiss of braking buses, white-noise chatter of voices, so many voices; a chorus of human sound. A woman walks past them, two screaming children in tow. Her face is red, her eyes thin, hands white where they clutch the handle of a buggy. Opposite them a slender man in a suit stops to tie his shoelace. Felix feels every ache, every strain on the stranger's face as he stoops slowly to the ground. Sensing he is watched, perhaps, the man looks up, and Felix turns quickly away.

"I stopped by after work one evening," he says, only half-conscious of the words coming from his mouth. "I think it was a Friday. I was tired."

"Sounds like a Friday to me." Michael's eyes seem to smile in the fading light. "Association."

"What does that mean?"

"It means that when we see angels, we think of Heaven and death. I bet there were lots of statues at Harriet's funeral."

"Yes," he says, remembering old, stony faces, smiling at him from the alcoves. "It was a church."

"Exactly. The church, the graveyard and the fact that this angel is a memorial shows you're associating these things with each other. She's reminding you of what happened, and how it affected you. It's normal to feel like this, Felix. Especially if you haven't dealt with what happened."

Across the street, at the bus stop, a small boy in football kit plays knee-ups with an empty beer can. He watches the boy, who seems smitten with the can, as though nothing in the world matters as much as keeping it from the ground. For one fleeting moment he admires the boy, who is so focused on such a small thing. Then he pities him, for the same reason. He pities them all; every man, every woman, every boy who could be contented with something as insignificant as an empty beer can; all of them lost in this city by the sea.

Chapter Twelve

On Friday night, as nearly every Friday night beforehand, Felix returns to the bar at Ocean Village. Michael says that it will help, that being around other people will make him feel better. Staring into the small, oval mirror above the sink while he brushes his teeth, he realises that he does not need persuading. If he has found any relief from life in the past five years, if he has glimpsed anything of what living used to mean before graduating, it has been at the bottom of a pint glass, or else swimming in the colourful depths of a cocktail. More than anything else, he needs that relief now; to feel reality wash away, and himself with it.

When they reach Ocean Village, they find Helen and Angela already waiting. The night is a vast, cloudless thing. They move slowly towards the bar, its warm light inviting them across the waterfront. Their footsteps echo in the dark, above which murmur their voices, and the elastic slap of the waves, soft but growing louder, as though excited by the promise of what is to come.

"It's not like you to be late," says Helen, as they mount the steps leading from the waterfront. Together the four of them make one long, amorphous silhouette, framed by the lights of the bar.

"Blame this one," says Michael, squeezing Felix's shoulders as he steers him through the night. "I'm always on time."

"Fashionably late," adds Felix.

"Are we in a hurry?" asks Angela, from the end of the line. "I mean, is there a rush?"

"No rush."

"Then it doesn't really matter."

Felix is surprised by the smile that tugs his cheeks. It

occurs to him that he knows very little about the woman walking beside him. Certainly there is nothing openly offensive about her. Quite the opposite; she carries herself with a quiet confidence that he realises is quite attractive. He will make an effort to get to know her better. Not because he should, he cautions himself, but because he wants to.

They begin the evening with a tray of Jack Rose; a sweet, syrupy cocktail that is all too easy to drink. Felix doesn't particularly enjoy the taste, but it doesn't last long and then they are laughing as they select a second round, fingertips tracing text across the menus. They try Moonwalk, and Midnight Dream, then a small, elegant glass of Paradise, and with each successive cocktail the bar becomes more blurry, the people less distinct around him, until he feels as though he might not be part of the room but merely observing it from an undefined point. He is all too familiar with the feeling.

"Down in one," he hears, from across the bar. Other voices slip into his ears, snippets of sentences, spoken then lost.

"What a week!"

"We'll go tomorrow. No looking back."

"I hate her, but I love her more. Does that make sense?"

The spotlights grow overhead, burning into the room, breaking apart where they hit spirit bottles, or the brightly-coloured liqueur glasses stacked behind the bar. The people, too, lose form; slowing and swaying as they move across the room, and it seems to him that their reflections move independently, a second shadow-bar mirrored in the glass doors to the smoking terrace, fragments of faces, races, light and colour captured in the smoke, the glass, the vast night. He studies these faces as they ghost against the dark and cannot help but notice that all of them are smiling, laughing, grinning; expressions unencumbered with concern of any sort at all. They are happy faces, and when he sees his own reflected there, and realises that he is among them, it is all he can do not to laugh out loud. The others are laughing too, even as they take his hand and pull him into the middle of the room.

To his left, a young woman moves against a man. Their legs press tightly together, as though slotting into place, while she shimmies slowly back and forth. Her fingers clasp tightly at his shirt, where it has slipped from out of his trousers. His hands are pressed firmly around her waist.

Behind them, two men are clasped in an embrace. With their arms wrapped tightly around each other's backs, they jump up and down beneath the spotlights. The men's faces are creased; eyes closed tight, teeth clamped together, lips set into smiles stretching from one side of their faces to the other. Just then, nothing in the world matters more than these expressions.

Through the press of people, Angela's hands find his. The room spins out of focus behind her until she is all that is left. His heart races to its own rhythm in his chest while his feet follow Angela's. Their palms grow hot and wet where they are joined.

He cannot remember the last time he danced like this. He knows only the lights, the heat, the music and Angela, smiling back at him with two rows of small, pearly teeth. She is beautiful in a plain, un-made-up kind of way. The loveliness of her lashes rise and fall with her eyelids when lights scatter across her face. Her dark brown eyes glitter when the same light catches them, like the wave-tips outside. An unfamiliar heat burns in his cheeks and under his arms, causing him to smile, stir, then look down and pull away. She holds tightly onto his hand.

Angela's wrists seem impossibly pale. With increasing concern, his eyes chase her thin arms to her body, naked and goose-pimpled with quills. She twists in response to the music, drawing him closer as more pinions rise from her skin, emerging like fledgling feathers from her flesh. Smatterings of coral cling to the shallow undersides of her breasts and beneath her arms. He follows the trail of growths up, past a narrow neck, and finds himself staring into the mad eyes of the angel.

Still, they dance wildly; he and this limp, pale thing in his arms. There is no breaking free, no escaping her hands at this point. His heart cannot race any faster. Even his smile does not fade, but seems to grow wider on his face until laughter rushes from his belly into his throat and out; a wild, meaningless sound, at once joyous and uncaring.

"The rain," she says, through a mouth that is both beak and lip. *"We love the rain. The water. We sing of it."*

He looks outside, past the bodies, the music, the lights, and realises that it is indeed raining. Water pours through the blackness, as though the night itself has grown wet and is running down the glass. Turning back to the angel, he laughs harder, tears filling his eyes.

"I'm waiting," she says. *"Beautiful voices. We're waiting."*

"No more waiting," he replies.

"Do you trust me, Felix?"

He tells her that he trusts her and she throws herself around him, enveloping him in feathers and bone.

They dance until they can no longer stand and then

they leave together. In a moment of lucidity, he watches Michael and Helen as they say their goodbyes and stumble into a taxi. Hand-in-hand, Angela and he brave the wet walk home. The city no longer seems to crush him. It is an ocean now; of glittering lights and damp air and dark dreams.

"I was born in the rain," he says enthusiastically to the woman on his arm. She shrieks, shielding herself beneath her bag as the two of them hurry through Queen's Park.

"I'm soaked through!" she says, still grinning in the dark.

"I thought you liked the rain?"

In her scrunched-up face he sees recognition. Removing the bag from above her head, she steps out of her shoes and runs ahead.

"Come on, Felix!" Her laughter fills the park.

He watches her as she runs, her small feet leaving long streaks in the mud. At first she is Angela; unknown, barely acquainted by drink and dance. Then she is the angel, fleeing through the night, feathers fluttering beneath her arms, and for a moment he hears screams again, like those of the gulls.

Then she is Harriet. He watches the small girl as she dashes through the trees, footprints tiny in the mud, hair streaming behind her, and feels pressure welling inside him as something pushes outwards, compelling him to move, to run after her through the rain, as he should have done that night. He realises that it is guilt, and that he has harboured it all these years; Dr. Moore's sea monsters, stirring in the deep.

***

The night melted around him, darkness lashing through

the air against his face. He had never seen so much water, never known such wetness, cold against his skin. His small, heavy heart rolled wildly in his chest. Behind him, Crows Hill blinked fast, beleaguered in the night. The hill became a waterfall of muddy movement. Ahead he saw the church spire, lit from within, shining like a lighthouse in the dark.

He stumbled up the hill towards the churchyard. Black water made a slide of the pathway. He hoped that Harriet was not there. He hoped that she had stayed at home, that she had seen sense; that for once she had listened to her parents and remained inside. Even as he thought these things, he knew that he would find her. There was no caution where Harriet was concerned. His words from earlier that day came back to him, as though he heard them again over the wind and rain.

"Harriet, I need to talk to you about something."

"So talk to me, then."

"I can't. Not here."

"Is it bad?"

"It's about me and my dreams. Please, I can't tell anyone else. It has to be you."

"Do you trust us, Felix?"

"What?"

She indicated the half-faced statues towering over them. "Do you trust us?"

"Yes. You're the only ones I trust."

"Then tell us now."

"Not now. Tonight, when everyone else is asleep. Let's say eleven o'clock."

"Fine. We'll meet back here. You can tell the angels, too. They're good at keeping secrets."

As he reached the top of the hill, he slipped to the

ground. Cold soaked his hands and knees. Struggling to his feet, he was afforded a view of the town below. A mixture of fear and fatigue knotted his stomach.

Blackness rushed towards Crows Hill, iridescent like crows' feathers or flowing silken sheets. The fields and hillsides ran, as though dissolving beneath the rain. Houses flickered and died, their lights extinguished by the water. More houses lit up as their owners awoke, only to blink and blackout. The town flashed feebly in the dark.

As he stood staring, a chorus of cries reached his ears. It was like no choir he was used to hearing. There was no righteousness or rhythm, only screams and shouts; human sounds made small by distance and the dark.

Turning from Crows Hill, he rushed towards the church. His legs burned but he forced them to keep moving. His heart sank as he saw the water pouring from gaps in the old wall. Grey stone shone white with wetness by the moon. Reaching the wall, he followed it to where it was the lowest, then climbed over, as Harriet had shown him, a dozen times before.

Stones slipped beneath his fingers, slimy and cold, like cobbled ice. Dragging himself over, he tumbled into the bushes. Water rushed into his nose and mouth. Sharp branches whipped across his face.

"Harriet!" he shouted. His voice sounded small beneath the wind. "Harriet!"

The water here was waist-deep. The same stone walls that let the water in were not so quick to let it out again. Soil lifted with the surface, which shone silvery black beneath the moonlight and with it a stagnant smell. He waded through it.

"Harriet! Harriet, are you here?"

"Felix!"

Stomach sinking, he chased after the voice. He called out. She shouted back. They played their sorry name game in the rain. As he followed after her voice, his eyes grew wet with fear.

"Harriet!"

"Felix!"

He found her by the statues, halfway between the gravestones and the church. He clung to a headstone, as she was clinging to an angel. Flood waters filled the clearing between them.

"Felix, the water. I can't swim."

The damp smelled worse here; ripe, almost rotten. Stepping towards her, he felt the tug of the current almost instantly. He dragged himself back around the headstone.

"Felix, help me –"

"Harriet, I can't –"

"Help me. Don't let me go."

Still pressed against the statue, she half turned, craning her neck towards the place where Felix stood. Their eyes met across the clearing. He had never seen Harriet look afraid before. He hadn't thought her capable of something like fear. She was his wild bird, his Siren, his friend, who ran through fields with him, and climbed trees, and laughed when no one else in Crows Hill dared to smile. He stared at her and she stared back at him, her eyes big and dark against her pale face.

"Don't let me go," she repeated, or he thought she did, because he couldn't hear her properly this time. Then she moved again, slipped, stuck out her hand and was gone beneath the black surface of the water.

Chapter Thirteen

In the darkness of his bedroom, Angela slowly removes her clothes. Visible as streaks of white in the city light through his window, she looks skeletal; a thin, hard shape with long bones for limbs. Naked, she slides into bed beside him.

As she begins to explore his body with her hands, he wishes that he could lose himself, as he lost himself at the bar. Her cold touch tickles the hairs down the back of his neck. They make love tenderly; a slow, reluctant kind of sex that turns his stomach. He wishes he could be sick, as though it would expel the badness from inside him; that he could continue being sick until his throat burned and everything went black and he found himself in that place Dr. Moore once warned him from, where there are tiny stars, and fish-faced figures swimming beside him, decay filling his nostrils like mouldering wood while scaled hands trace across his arms and legs, slick and silvery in the darkness –

He wakes the next morning entangled in her arms. Quietly he moves from beside her. Stepping from the bed, he dresses quickly. It is still dark outside, the sky deep indigo blue. As he hunts for his jeans, he notices her muddy clothes, in a pile by the bed, her bare footprints black against the floorboards, the chain hanging from the latch, where he forgot to lock it. He feels violated in a way he could never openly admit. Not by the softly-sleeping shape beneath his bed covers, but by himself. It is the ultimate step in social obligation; to drink, to pick someone up, bring them home and sleep with them. He feels betrayed by the bar, where for one night a week he thought that he was free from these obligations. Mostly, he does not want what has happened.

He leaves a mug out in the kitchen, beside a spoon and his last teabag. Beneath the mug he places a note, explaining nothing really at all. Then he leaves his flat and walks the short distance through the city. The streets are still littered with Friday night.

Walking past a convenience store, he stares through the rain-speckled window at the contents. Chocolate glistens in translucent packets, beside which bulge vast bags of sweets, bloated and bright like jellyfish. Vestigial raindrops veer down the glass, breaking the colours behind so that they blur, running into one another, painting a picture of kaleidoscopic chaos.

Further down the high street he notices properly a number of other shop windows, similarly distorted by the rain. Inside the window of a women's clothes shop, three mannequins weep silent tears, their empty eyes fixed lidless on his. Scarves snake around their necks like shining eels, while floral scrunchies bloom by their small feet; fat mounds of cutting-fashion coral. Beside the clothes shop is a window filled with mobile phones, all of them voiceless on their stands; empty shells, lavish models suggesting luxury and perhaps langoustine limbs, barely concealed inside the husks.

Hurrying down the rest of the high street, he comes to a stop before the statue. She stares over him, surveying her city. Standing in the shadow of East Park, he feels none of the fear or anxiety he felt before. She has shown him her worst. He can sink no lower. He feels very little of anything since leaving the bar the night before. If he experienced an hour of true happiness drinking and dancing, then he is prised open now; plundered, left broken at the bottom of the sea, where all things that are dropped or die or cannot swim eventually settle.

If he looks into the sky he can still see the stars,

winking as they are swallowed slowly by dawn. Pink blossom blows from East Park around the statue.

"It's my fault," he says. "It's my fault Harriet's gone. She drowned because of me. She liked the rain too. I think you probably had a lot in common. She says you used to play with her. Her smiling statues. I don't know if that was you, or if she was making it all up. I don't suppose it matters. We first spoke to each other in hymn practice. Matthew Petty had stolen my verse sheet…"

Sinking to the floor beside the memorial, he crosses his legs, huddles into his coat and continues talking. He tells the statue about that morning at hymn practice, and Harriet's voice, which was so much like he imagined a Siren's voice to be. He tells her about the other boys at school, about how they ignored him and how lonely he was. He tells her about the dreams he used to have; the bullying, the loneliness, the bird-faced children in the locker-room. Then he talks about how Harriet made all of it go away.

He talks until the city stirs, announced by lively birdsong and the moan of waking traffic. People begin to walk past him, although not many. He does not hear these things, or see them, in any clear sense. He is aware of very little except his memories, spilling like waves from his mouth, growing lighter and less forceful with every lap from his tongue until their tide is spent, foam fading, his body hollow, and he knows relief.

Chapter Fourteen

Felix moves through crowds, down streets, past cars and trees, which line the walk by East Park. Blossom burgeons through the leaves, reminding him that even in this bright, grey place there is the soft promise of life, and that the city stands on the doorstep of the New Forest. Not a dozen miles away he might find himself in the dank, shining hollows of those trees, where worms turn in the soil and fruit swells on the branch. There is life in the city, and beside it. He sees that now.

For the first time in months, the prospect of Monday morning is not entirely unwelcome. Sitting at his desk, he marvels at the mediocrity of it all. It doesn't matter that he does not enjoy his job because he is not here to enjoy himself. He is here to work, like the rest of the city's residents when they drag themselves from bed to make their morning commutes. He has been living in a dream, haunted by guilt, but now the guilt is gone.

Movement outside makes him turn, and for a moment he imagines a ruined figure stalk past the window. Then he sees the long, black coat for what it is, the grey work trousers, his friend's face, made more pointed by his restrained hair, and something that resembles a smile tugs Felix's cheeks. As Mr. Coleson greets Michael at the door, the smile turns into a laugh.

"Bastard," says Michael, when Felix and he are able to speak properly three hours later. Planting his hands on the desk, he leans in close. Felix feels the word more than he hears it; a syllabic bite in his heart.

"Excuse me?"

"Not you. Coleson."

"Poetic," says Felix, logging off and standing from his chair. He stretches, then shakes his arms until he feels vaguely human again. They wander outside, where he waits while Michael lights up. "In his defence, you're a terrible employee."

"I resent that comment."

"Come on, you're always late."

"I'm never late to drinks."

"No, that's my job. You're late to work, though."

"And who's been having a better time of it lately, out of the two of us?"

The road outside their office passes Felix by, figures blurring as they lurch across the pavement. Michael takes a long, crisp drag on his cigarette. Seeming to realise what he's said, his arm finds Felix's waist and sits there. "Sorry. Blame Monday morning. I didn't mean that."

Pigeons twitch on the roadside, wings flapping, bodies flocking, a swarm of grey growing larger then smaller, like a puddle in the sun. Clouds blend into each other before speeding away, falling like fast-forwarded snow through the sky. The very pavement beneath Felix's feet grows longer, thinner, stretching far into the distance until it seems like the only thing keeping him from falling into the racing concrete river is Michael's arm, the grip of his fingers through his shirt.

"Felix?"

Blinking, he comes to himself again.

"Felix? You in there?"

"Yes, sorry. What?"

Michael exhales slowly, smoky breath blowing around his face. "I said sorry, that's all. Let's eat."

The quiet bar and the promise of two seats at a table outside draw them to a small pub near the end of London Road. They order quickly; bottled beers, a bowl of spiced king prawns and two steak burgers. The day has grown warmer since Felix walked to work that morning. Sunlight shines persistently over the city, piercing clouds in the heavenly fashion that suggests it may yet later rain through the brightness. He realises he is smiling. Half-shielding his eyes, he browses a spare menu.

"You look good today."

"Thanks," says Felix, "I think."

"I mean better than you have been looking. Like you've slept."

"I'm feeling a little better. And I have slept. All weekend, really."

"No dreams?"

"No dreams. I think you were on to something when you talked about association."

Michael stares at him a moment longer before he is forgotten in favour of the surrounding street. He follows Michael's gaze to the kerb, where two pigeons are scratching for crumbs from a nearby bin.

The side-order arrives; crimson seafood drizzled with oil and herbs. They each help themselves to a plump prawn, and while they eat he tells Michael about what he felt at the bar on Friday, about Angela and what had followed.

"You're welcome," says Michael, when he is finished.

"For your advice?"

"For Angela."

Looking up from the table, he sees Michael's lips, stretched into a long smile as they slide around a slippery prawn. He follows suit, his mouth filling with garlic and grease.

"It shouldn't have happened."

"But it did," says Michael.

"Not like that."

"But it did."

He looks back out over London Road. The street is busying with lunchtime traffic. The pigeons are fighting over a piece of sesame bun, pecking desperately at the bread, flicking it skywards with quick snaps of their beaks. Women wobble past on heels too high while men with faces shaven clean stride briskly in their wake. His thoughts turn to Sam, one day living his life as best he can, the next sitting wretched beside the street; swallowed by dark gutters, labyrinthine alleys down which entire lives are lost, flooded with shining shadows against which no man can swim until he is weak and prey to thin winged things, which hover in the sky, men's fears made flesh and blood and feathered bone –

"It helped," he says, plucking another prawn from the bowl. "It helped to talk about Harriet, and what happened."

"Sometimes that's all it takes. I would imagine statues make great listeners."

"I meant you, actually."

"Well, that's what I'm here for."

"Seriously."

"I'm being serious. I'm glad you're feeling better."

Their burgers arrive and they busy themselves with eating. For a few minutes nothing else matters except the scrape of their knives through thick steak, the crunch of crisp chips between their teeth, the saltiness of their meals, which so complements the saltiness of the sea air in the city where Felix has made his home and, for the first time in years, feels as though he might belong.

"Are you going to see Angela again?"

"We should get back soon. Coleson will have your head on a spike."

"Don't care," says Michael, swallowing back his last mouthful of steak. "It's just a job. Are you going to see her again?"

"It's complicated."

"It's as complicated as you make it, Felix. Take her out. Call her, arrange a date. Make the most of this, before it starts raining again." He raises his beer in celebration of the sun, face twisting, eyes closing in discomfort as he turns them to the light. In the bowl on the table between them, Felix fancies he sees the last prawn shiver; a sad langoustine ghost in its oily grave. "Because it will rain again. Especially here, in this place where the city and the sea make messy love."

Chapter Fifteen

The museum is not far from Felix's block of flats. He has passed the old building, which had once been a medieval warehouse, many times before when walking between his flat and Leisure World. He even visited once, when still a student with the university. A paper on local history led him to the museum; the final resting place of some of the material objects salvaged from the icy waters, the night the RMS Titanic went down.

Crossing the road past the convenience shop, he takes an alleyway, bringing him parallel to what remains of the old city walls. The ruins are among the oldest parts of the city to have survived the bombing that otherwise levelled Southampton during the Second World War. A sense of restfulness fills the air, a quiet detachment, which he finds both soothing and strange, as though the past is bleeding slowly into this moment. He thinks of blood and the sea and the city that has bathed in both. Southampton suffered greatly at the hands of that conflict. Looking at the later architecture, which has risen in place of the destruction, he does not think it ever really recovered; a city scarred by fire and screams, its citizens reduced to ruin and ghosts. If it is true man must surround himself with images of Heaven, it is also true he cannot live without reminders of death. He finds himself wondering if the two are not the same.

When he reaches the museum, it is closed. A sign informs him that it has been relocated to the city centre. Anxiety stirs inside him, and he worries that he has made a mistake listening to Michael, that this is an omen he should not meet Angela again; Old Town telling him to turn back, to walk away from this woman and go home. The thought is tempting, except that they have already arranged to meet and he will not leave anyone waiting again.

The city is heaving with weekend traffic. When he called Angela at the start of the week, Saturday had seemed like the best day on which to meet. Mostly he was relieved that she had said yes, and gave little thought to something as trivial as the time. They both worked during the week anyway, and neither of them had known when the museum closed on weekdays. As he steps around yet another group of shoppers, he remembers in no uncertain terms why it is advisable to remain indoors on Saturdays.

Taking a side-street, he walks up Portland Terrace, where the tide of pedestrians is weaker. Bold, blue banners announce the museum and the woman standing beside it. He moves between the banners, down the flagstone path to where he can see Angela waiting. She is dressed casually in a pair of denim jeans and a stylish black thin-knit jumper.

"Sorry I'm late." They hug briefly, her arms finding the small of his back. The jumper is soft against his hands. Overhead, the banners whip in the sea breeze. "I went to the wrong place. It's moved since I was last here."

"About two years ago, yes." She stares at him a second longer, her eyes interrogatory, then smiles. "I'm sorry too. For the other week. I should have called, you should have called. We could play the blame game all day. Clean slate?"

"Clean slate."

Turning, she surveys the outside of the building. Seeing her small silhouette framed by the towering building, Felix feels strangely humbled. When she turns back to him, her smile has resurfaced. "You know, I've always wanted to come here."

There is a small fee at the entrance. He pays for their admission, after which they find themselves in a long corridor. They move through the entrance hall, towards the galleries. A tall ceiling hangs over them, supported by rows of broad pillars. Standing beneath the spotlights, he thinks of tombs made bright and modern.

Faded photographs line the walls of the first room, blown up for clarity. There are couples, and lonely children, some in smart dress, others wrapped up warm against the sea; men and women from all walks of turn-of-the-century life. They share the same story; survivors or the families of those who were not so fortunate. One frame shows five boys in flat caps, standing together on a school playing field. Another features a young girl in a simple plaid dress, a bear tucked beneath one arm. She stares down from the photograph, not quite at Felix but through him, and he wonders whether there should be a mother and father in the empty spaces by her side.

He spends a long time studying one young man in particular. His features are sharp, with prominent cheeks and searching eyes, and Felix finds himself speculating who this man was. Not his name, which is printed underneath the photograph, but his identity, and what brought him to the Titanic for her maiden voyage.

"He's handsome," says Angela behind his shoulder. "It's so sad."

"He lived."

"Maybe, but lots of others didn't."

Staring up at the man, he realises Angela is right. He wonders how it is this man lived through the disaster, and why he lived when so many others did not. He was a man with a face and a name, no better or worse than any of the other men, women or children who stepped proudly, unknowing, onto the ship that afternoon, and did not step off again.

The next gallery is filled with cabinets. They take their time studying what they can of the contents. There is far too much to see in one afternoon. Angela lingers by some broken whalebone combs, which might once have lived on an expensive dressing table, before finding themselves returned to the depths of their natural element. He examines a pocket watch in the cabinet beside them. The object is tiny, its face set inside tarnished brass. The hands are missing, but there are shadows of the hands against the yellowing watch face, suggesting the time it stopped when its owner fell and was consumed by the waves. So much time was taken that night; entire lives snuffed out in the depths.

"You've wanted to come here for a while, then?" asks Felix.

"I visited the old museum, when it was still by the docks. But I was very young. I haven't been since it relocated here."

"Did your family lose anyone?"

"Not that I know of. It was so long ago. But I feel still attached to what happened."

"I suppose a lot of people do. Because of the city and the part it played."

"You would think so." Her voice echoes around the room.

While they wander the rooms together, they talk. It is a long time since he has taken anyone out and her gentle inquiries are perhaps more apparent to him than they should be. He uses the opportunity to return her questions.

Aside from a short interval at Royal Holloway in London, where she too studied History, Angela has always lived in Southampton. She loves the city. That much is obvious from the way that she describes its streets, its distinctions; the kinds of nuances a person would only notice if they were looking through appreciative eyes. They talk about Old Town, where he had found himself wandering aimlessly not an hour earlier; about the cobbled pavements that still exist outside some of the buildings, the crumbling walls and the hush that hangs over the place, surprising for somewhere that has seen so much blood and death. She did her third-year dissertation on the history of the zone, and feels well-versed in its past.

"It's a graveyard without the graves," she says. "You can sense what has happened there, even without headstones to inform you who died and when."

"I didn't think anyone else noticed these things."

"I don't think many people do."

In the last room, among the cabinets and artefacts, Felix catches sight of a familiar face, staring back at him from a photograph across the room.

"The angel," he says, drawn immediately to the display. Newspaper cut-outs date back to the first unveiling of the statue in 1914, and faded photographs from the same day, and a dozen clearer images, taken more recently. The weight of the angel's significance hangs over him.

"Nike," states Angela.

"Sorry?"

"It's not an angel. It's Nike, the Greek goddess of Victory, blessing the engineers for remaining at their posts while the ship sank."

"I didn't know."

"It's an easy mistake to make. If you see her as an

angel, then that's what matters. She's kind of a classical antecedent of the angel anyway."

Choosing one of the clearer documents, detailing the script on the memorial plaque, Angela begins to read aloud. Together their fingers follow the lines of text through the glass.

> *GREATER LOVE HATH NO MAN THAN*
> *THIS. THAT A MAN LAY DOWN HIS*
> *LIFE FOR HIS FRIENDS*
> *ST. JOHN 15TH CH. 13TH V*
> *TO THE MEMORY OF THE ENGINEER OFFICERS*
> *OF THE R.M.S "TITANIC" WHO SHOWED*
> *THEIR HIGH CONCEPTION OF DUTY AND THEIR*
> *HEROISM BY REMAINING AT THEIR POSTS*
> *15TH APRIL 1912.*

Angela's finger catches up with his on the glass. For a second they touch, shivers trickling like cold water down his neck. Then she withdraws her hand, and he smiles, and they wander slowly back through the gallery.

"Well, that was emotional."

"Sorry," he says. "I'm not very good at this."

"The reading. It's an emotional inscription."

"Oh, yes."

"I'm sure the words don't do it justice. I can't imagine how frightened they must have been. Not just the engineers, but everyone. Watching the water rise around them like that."

He dares to think he understands. Not the Titanic specifically, but the nature of the fear Angela describes; to have the world spin around you, to see the fear of life and death in a person's eyes, to watch water and sky become one vast fabric, a fine skin against which presses human distress, lively with flailing arms and kicking legs and icy breath –

"Some of them saw Death," she says, as they pass back through the first room. "They really believed they saw him, you know, floating beside them in the sea."

"Fear makes people see strange things."

The faces in the photographs watch them as they return through the gallery. They pass the young man again, and the small girl with her bear, and the dozens of others staring but not seeing from their mounts on the walls. Spotlights guide them towards the exit.

"For the record, Felix, you are good at this."

"There was a flood," he reveals, "when I was a child. I was there, in the middle of it. I suppose it's given me some insight –"

"Not this," she interrupts, nodding towards one of the photographs. "This. I'm really enjoying myself."

He glances from the picture frame down to his hand, where her fingers have found his again. Silence floods the museum. Then, despite himself, he looks back to the image on the wall. For a moment he isn't sure what he is seeing. When he can't quite believe what his eyes are showing him, he takes an uncertain step closer. Angela's hand slips from his as coldness descends the small discs of his spine.

"Felix?"

It is the photograph of the five boys in the flat caps. The boys are smiling, but their faces are changed. Loose flesh hangs from beneath their chins. Black eyes stare madly into his from above beak-mouths, their features brought to life in limp wattle and old bone.

"Felix, what is it?"

Stepping back from the photograph, he hears the shrieks of the boys as they flock from the playing fields. He feels the compressing blackness of the locker room, as though he is there again, alone in the darkness. The room brims with the smell of brine, and with a nauseating lurch he finally recognises what it is that has been haunting him.

"I have to leave."

"What is it? What's the matter?"

Beside the photograph of the boys, the skinny figure of the girl with the bear studies him with bulbous eyes the colour of bruised fruit. Downy feathers emerge like fur down her thin arms. On the next wall, an elderly woman screams from behind talon-hands, gums pink where they are visible between black lips. The man with the striking features withers before Felix's eyes, wasting away to feathers and bone, staring at him with a face that seems to smile.

"Felix, what's happened?"

"I have to go."

He turns from the paintings to Angela, catching sight of the pale face at her shoulder as he does so. He barely glimpses it before it is gone again, but it is long enough to recognise the scrawny figure standing behind her, its expression pained, wide mouth gaping beside her ear.

"Felix?"

"I'm sorry."

Running from the museum, he might be twelve again; a small boy fleeing from a town he did not recognise, from a life he did not understand. It is many years since he dreamed of the bird-boys. Not since leaving Crows Hill has he given them a thought. Dr. Moore was supposed to have made him safe from them, but it is clear now that they have survived with him, in some shape and form.

Streets spill into the pavements that once marked them, forming endless rivers of dark grey. Buildings blur beneath the skyline, which seems to sag, then sinks beneath the sheer weight of water pressing down on it.

At some point across the city, he does not know when for sure, the crescendo of sound breaks, or perhaps it is he that breaks under the sound, unable to listen a second longer. Perhaps he wonders, he broke a long time ago, and has been cracking ever since; the real rupturing like an eggshell, now broken around him, sticky and wet with albumen. He hears only white noise now. It might be a high-pitched ringing in his ears, or one long, avian scream.

Halfway down East Street, he slips down an alley to catch his breath. The alleyway is narrow, his world spinning, and his speed carries him into a plastic waste disposal bin. The tall black bin rocks on its wheels before finally losing balance and toppling over. He stumbles away from it into the wall as rubbish scatters across the ground.

At first it is impossible to tell what it is that spills from the bin. He recognises organs, orifices and glittering shells, like a rash of coral across the ground. He imagines he sees shellfish among the stew, and sticky, feathered shapes. Filled with a fascinated revulsion, he studies the floundering forms and the bin from which they spill, which seems to contain no bottom, no base, only a deep, singular blackness.

There are bones in the debris; some bare, others with strips of pale meat still gripping them, and things that are more skin than bone, with eyes and yawning mouths, all of them carried in a grey liquid, which ebbs across the street into the gutter. Last to leave the mouth of the bin is a malformed shape, pulling itself into the alley. It flops pitifully onto the pavement, arms flapping weakly in the air as it seeks to right itself.

Goosebumps prick his skin, his ears and nose numb. His arms shiver by his sides as the oceanic slime laps at his shoes. He can feel it on his skin and under it; a deep blanket that could swallow him up and save him from the rest of the world, if he would only let it. The water is a part of him, from the moment he was born, screaming, into the flood of '88, to the night it took Harriet from the arms of the angels, to here, now, in this city that was built by the sea and has endured, through bombs and blood and human madness. Michael's words come back to him through the soft slaps of the waves against the docks.

"It's this world, this life. It nurtures dreams, like a force of nature."

***

"Let me tell you about dreams, Felix," said Dr. Moore one morning, when he came to Felix's room after breakfast. With his father's permission, Felix had spent the night in the great house where the doctor lived and worked, so that his sleeping patterns could be studied. Like the rest of the house, the bedroom was musty, filled with still air. The wallpaper might have been white once but had become an off-beige, whether from age or some other internal ailment he couldn't tell. Pastel curtains complemented the blandness, between which sat a vase of tired-looking roses. It was a bright morning; Dr. Moore's old, round face illuminated in the light by the window.

"I would really like to go home now, please."

"Soon, Felix."

"How soon is soon?"

"As soon as you're feeling better. Your father is worried about you."

"I don't want him to be worried. I'm fine. I told him I was strong."

"You're very strong. I can tell. But sometimes even strong people need help. That is where I come in. Tell me, now, have you ever seen the sea?"

"No." He shook his head.

"Never?"

"Father used to say he would take me, one day."

"Well, isn't that something? I grew up beside it. A small town, on top of white cliffs. It wasn't warm, not like it sometimes gets here in the summer, but on bright days, when the wind allowed, I would occasionally walk the cliff-tops with my mother. I can still remember the coldness of the air in my face. The sounds of the water as it heaved its bulk over and over against the rocks. And the waves… You will never see anything so humbling as the sea, Felix."

"I've read about it. In school."

"Good, good. Imagine for me a sea, then. A vast body of water, so great that no shores are visible, only the deep, singular blue of the water and the sky. Sometimes this blue is calm, a stretch of sea undisturbed by wind or rain or anything at all, except small waves, which leap and shiver with life. When a person sleeps, he floats through this sea and the waves form shapes around him. The feeling is quite awesome, in the proper sense of the word. There is no escaping the sea, into which we must all fall when we sleep.

"A calm sea goes forgotten, the dreamer unknowing. He wakes with only the vaguest memories; of faces, or pale shapes seen in the water, at which he shakes his head and rubs his eyes and yawns these lingering things into oblivion."

At first Felix didn't understand what Dr. Moore was talking about. Then he realised he had no reason to doubt this man, who was both a professional and his father's friend. He was reminded of Odysseus, drifting peacefully to distant ports surrounded by the gentle slap of water and the sun. He shared this comparison.

"Yes, you are quite right. I remember his travels well, from my own studies as a boy. But just as Odysseus sailed on still seas, Felix, he also encountered waves that were fierce. Winds battered his sails and monsters from the deep rose to snap at ship and men alike.

"This was his Odyssey, and like his Odyssey, there are dreams that are not safe. These dreams are terrifying things, dragging darkness with them, and the cold. The shapes that form in these waters rise from cities of sunken spires to devour the dreamer whole. They are dreams of the self, and of other things as old as man, and older still. They steal the very breath from the dreamer's lungs until he sinks into the blackness beneath them, small and alone in an ocean of fear, never waking, never fighting, until he really does wake, sometimes shouting, or thrashing in his covers, and finds his daytime thoughts turned dark and rotten. Such dreams change people. Over time they twist them, altering them in ways they do not even realise. That is why it is important we address your dreams, so that they do not take you over, and you remain Felix."

***

He does not know why the bird-figure is reappearing now. He imagines it growing with him, limbs lengthening, back breaking, feathers sprouting from beneath its tattered arms even as he himself grew into adulthood; a twisted symbiote, a fowl host, feeding on his fears as it had once fed on those of a frightened boy.

His eyes scrunch shut. He listens to his pulse, thumping in his ears. Coldness from the brick wall seeps into his palms, and when he opens his eyes again there is only the alleyway, like a deep-sea chasm beneath a sliver of light, which could be the sky or the sea. Struggling for breath, he sinks against his frame, and considers again the simplicity of slipping, sleeping, into this light and not waking.

Chapter Sixteen

It is over a year since Felix has visited Michael's house but his feet still remember the way. He used to come here often, when Michael first moved into the property. After graduating he was surprised to find himself unaccustomed to independence. University was preparation for life, they said, except there were no lectures on living, nothing to tell him how or why he should go on, or hint at where he might end up.

He passes a garden, in which a dog, chained to a post, cries like a hungry gull, then he is standing outside a house. He stares up at the building, with its drawn curtains, its crumbling brick and overgrown garden, a residential reflection of more than just Miserly Road, before lifting the latch on the gate and walking up to the porch. The door is black, in keeping with everything else he has seen of the street, and the night sky above it.

As he presses his finger to the bell, a weight of relief washes through him. He has never been happier to see Michael's house, or the silhouette of his friend, visible through the foggy glass in the front door.

The kitchen is a bright, modern place, clean-cut with sharp corners. Felix finds himself on a tall, metal stool, slumped over a bowl of cereal. His spoon dips in and out of the milk while Michael finds them each a beer. The floating wheat flakes form a misshapen face, smiling up at him from the table.

"One for you," says Michael, his head emerging from the fridge, "and one for me."

Felix pushes the grinning cereal to one side and takes the bottle presented to him. The brown glass feels cold, and wet with condensation. He takes a sip, swallows, then sobs into his hand.

"I'm going mad."

"You're not going mad."

"The world, then. The world is going mad, and I'm the only one who seems to see it. I felt fine, this week. After visiting the statue, I felt better. But I'm not."

Michael stares at him a moment longer, then takes a brisk swig of his beer. Pulling up a second stool, he positions himself next to Felix. His aftershave fills Felix's face; a familiar smell from a hundred taxi rides after a hundred evenings spent beside the sea. The scent settles comfortably in his nose.

"Do you remember that night in East Park, after Rachel had broken up with me?"

Felix recalls the night well. It was almost dawn when Michael and he had found themselves by the docks. They had wandered the city for hours. Their path had taken them from their student house in Portswood, through London Road into Southampton proper. It was one of the first times Felix had walked the night-time city sober.

They remained by the sea for almost an hour that night, talking, and listening to the supple slaps of the waves, before retracing their steps through the city. It was then, as they sought to avoid the clubs and pubs turning out for the night, that they found themselves in East Park. The street lights still persisted, poking their heads through the tree-tops, but it was quieter there, more peaceful behind the branches. At the time, that seemed important.

"Yes," Felix says, staring back at Michael beside him in the kitchen. "I remember."

"Rachel Lowe. She meant a lot to me, that one, and when she left, she took more than she knew with her."

"What did she take?"

"I'm not sure exactly, but it was something important. She was everything, and then she was nothing, but I was still here. Left behind. That's what it means to be mad. To be stripped of meaning, stripped so bare you feel like the skin's been torn from your back and you're just bones. Bare bones and nerves, stuck out in the cold, where it stings, it burns like nothing you've felt before."

Michael's words wash through him as another sob bubbles up from his chest. He feels giddy; light-headed with relief. "You understand."

"Of course I understand. And do you know why I wasn't lost completely, wandering through the city that night? Because you were there. We sat by that memorial and we talked, about everything except Rachel, and you showed me that life went on without her. I don't think you meant to, but you did. You were there beside me in the dark, Felix, so no matter how lost you feel, or how mad the world gets, or how dark, I'll always be here too."

His eyes are burning, the kitchen swimming out of focus around him. He drinks until his bottle of beer is empty and then he goes to sleep. Michael makes him a bed on the sofa.

"I'm in the next room if you need anything," he seems to say, as Felix fades from wakefulness into what follows after. Michael's smiling face blurs above him. "Stay as long as you need. I'll square everything with work. Now try to sleep."

He spends the rest of the week at Miserly Road. In the mornings he tidies the house, and occasionally walks to the nearby shops in Woolston. The suburb is quieter than the Southampton he is familiar with, more distant, but still recognisable as part of the city in a strange, peripheral way. As he walks through its streets, he notices a kind of decay across the houses and gardens, the sort that is associated with all things marginal. The houses seem too tall, or squat, while others belong to a war-time city, or look even older. He studies crumbling wooden beams, walls flecked with smatterings of stones, and windows that seem to stare back at him; glassy sockets watching helplessly as the outside world passes them by. He wonders if he looks so different himself.

It is both true and it is not. There are similarities between him and these ghost houses, yes; namely the sense of infringement he feels, lingering inside him. He expects that he will always feel this. He has stared too long into the abyss, filled with its shifting blackness and the distant flutter of wing beats. There is no coming back from such contemplation.

But he is not completely lost. Tenuous links still tether him to the city and the people who give it its eyes, its breath, its fingers, fumbling blindly through the night. He has a job, if not a career. There are people who depend on him, however loosely. He has Michael.

More than once during these walks he finds himself thinking about Sam. It is not uncommon for Felix to go weeks without encountering him around the city, but he had not seemed himself when they last spoke. Wherever he is, Felix hopes he is safe. He can't imagine what he would do without his flat to return home to each evening, without Michael to drink with and depend on. It occurs to him that there is one place left he might check, if not for Sam himself then for knowledge of the man's whereabouts, and peace of mind. Before he really knows what he is doing, he finds himself walking away from Woolston towards the city.

Sometimes he finds himself staring into space, as

though he is looking not at the trees, the sky, the various houses that line the roads, but through these things. He remembers his conversations with Dr. Moore as a child, and fancies he sees other things behind the streets, as though they are the surface of an ocean; its waves rearing then crashing around him, and beneath them is another place, where dreams swim with fish amid sunken cities and drowned angels dance through the depths.

***

"And how are we today, Felix?"

The beige walls of the doctor's study filled his eyes, the faintly-patterned curtains, the flowers; fierce red this time, refreshed since they had last spoken.

"I'm feeling better, thank you."

"Good, very good. And your dreams?"

"What about them?"

"When we last spoke, you told me about the bird-boys in the locker room. You said that when you met and became friendly with Harriet, these dreams diminished, but that they were beginning to manifest themselves again, now that she is gone."

"Yes," said Felix. "I see them all the time."

"And how do these dreams make you feel?"

"Lonely."

"And how else do they make you feel?"

Felix remembered scarlet wattle, smooth skin and a heat, which seemed to burn him up from inside and set fire to his cheeks. "Excited."

"I thought as much. Remember what I said before, comparing dreams to seas and how they could swallow men whole? That is what these dreams will do."

"I can't help it. I don't mean to dream about Matthew

and the other boys –"

"They are exciting, you say. But this must be frightening, too?"

"Yes."

"Concentrate on that. Remember how much they frighten you. Things frighten us for good reason. They frighten us because they are dangerous. Because they can hurt us. Change us."

"So I should ignore the dreams?"

"Yes. You must ignore them. And you must not tell anyone else about them."

"But when I thought I could tell Harriet, I felt better."

"And look what happened to her, Felix. The things you are dreaming about are not healthy. They will make you different from the other boys. Is that what you want?"

"No…"

"Then fight them! You are a clever young man, I can see that. Tell me, how did Odysseus overcome the Sirens and their song?"

"His men tied him to the ship's mast. We learned about it with Mr. Stuart."

"That is what I am doing. I am tying you to a mast, so that you will not succumb to these bird-boys and the dream on which they fly."

***

It is a long walk from Woolston into the city centre, and the sea breeze turns his skin to goose flesh. Standing in the long shadow of the Church of Holy Waters, he tells himself it will be different to when he last visited. This is a place of sanctuary, if not for him, then for Sam.

The foyer is vacant. The air is still cold, but drier and vaguely dusty. The corridors either side are also unoccupied, and for a moment he imagines the entire church is empty, before noticing that the doors to the service hall are ajar. Entering the heart of the church, he spots a solitary man at the far end, in the pulpit. He appears to be packing some books away into a worn leather bag as Felix approaches.

"You look lost."

"I'm sorry," says Felix, reaching the altar, "I'm not sure if I should be in here or not."

The man smiles sadly. "You misunderstand. I mean you look *lost*."

A strange feeling comes over Felix, as though the lights grow brighter where they stream in through the windows, the shadows darker between the pews and in the alcoves. He feels the man's wet eyes on him, hears the breath of the ocean as it echoes through the room, fancies movement in the windows; angels and demons playing out eternal battle in the glass. The pressure builds until it becomes too much and he has to speak.

"Are you the vicar?"

"Mark Thomas. How can I help you?"

In his plain clothes the vicar appears quite ordinary. He might be in his sixties, although Felix has never been very good with ages. Felix guesses he is of his father's generation, if not from his hair then his ruddy face, hinting at a taste for more than communion wine.

"I'm looking for someone. A friend. He used to come here, I think. I wondered if you might have seen him recently."

Stepping down from the pulpit with an armful of books, the vicar extends what he can of a hand. They shake briefly. "Let's see. Does this friend have a name?"

"A few," says Felix, smiling. "Sam, probably."

"And his surname?"

"I'm not sure. He would have come here for a roof over his head. He didn't like the shelters."

"Ah, yes. Draper." The vicar leads him to the front row of pews. They each take a seat, the old wood groaning beneath their weight.

Even inside the church, Felix realises he can hear the tide. There are other sounds too; the patter of claws, or tiny feet, skittering through the rafters. "Can you hear that?"

"The gulls," explains the vicar. "They nest, somewhere above us. It is an old building, sadly falling into disrepair. Funding is not so forthcoming, recently."

If the architecture reminds Felix of anywhere else, it is Oxford, with its brooding colleges and haughty spires. He wonders how the rest of Southampton might look today, had it not once been bombed so heavily. The vicar appears to read his thoughts.

"It's beautiful, isn't it?"

"Yes. There's a church where I grew up but it's nothing like this. A small building, for a small town."

"We were lucky to survive the war. All of this could have been lost. The windows, the stonework, the angels in the alcoves…"

"What do they want?"

"I'm sorry?"

"The angels," says Felix, surprised by his own directness. "What are they? What do they want?"

"They are messengers. I would imagine they want the same thing that we all want."

"And what is that?"

"To be loved. And to return that love in kind."

"By God, you mean?"

A wistful smile flits over the vicar's face. "I occasionally joke that they love the water. That they sing of it, and that if my parishioners listen carefully when it rains, they might hear the angels' voices in the sky."

"Sam says that sometimes."

"Yes, of course. Sam Draper." While the vicar speaks, he resumes packing the books into his bag. "I run a group, once a week, for the homeless. He would join us, from time to time. We're talking about the same man?"

Felix takes a moment to organise his thoughts. It is a slippery few seconds, in which dreams, memories and waking terrors wash over each other in his head.

"Yes, I think that's him."

"I'm afraid I haven't seen him for some time now. Not since his birthday, a few weeks ago. Some of the others from the shelter came. We had tea, and I made coffee cake, although I can't say it tasted very much of coffee, or cake for that matter." The vicar pauses, Bible in hand. Then he deposits the book into his rucksack. "Yes, it would be weeks since he was last here. It's not unusual, for a man in his position, but you do worry, of course."

"His birthday?"

"Yes, at least, that's what he said. His thirtieth."

Something moves in the rafters. The scratching intensifies, and Felix imagines a shape in the overhead gloom. As he watches, the figure leans forward; peering down from the beams, and then it is toppling through the space between the ceiling and the floor. There is nothing graceful about its descent. It falls heavily, flapping like a bundle of old clothes before crashing soundlessly into the pews.

"I'm sorry," says the vicar, unseeing. Beside him, the broken figure twitches silently where it lies on the stone floor. Felix witnesses bones, matted plumage, and, staring back from beneath a splintered arm, the gaunt suggestion of a man's smiling face. Swallowing, he turns away.

"Thank you."

Chapter Seventeen

Friday flaps frantically at the windows, but Felix does not open the door to it. He thinks of little all day except the vicar's words, and the shivering sack of bones on the church floor beside him. Only a few years older than he, Sam is alone in the world, except for the angel beside whom he sometimes sleeps and begs. It is no wonder a moment with her in the storm-tossed skies seems preferable to this absurd life. Felix feels as though he is living underwater, in this city where the air smells of salt; sinking deeper and deeper with each passing day into the crushing oblivion of life's depths.

"What a week," says Michael, when he returns from the office in the evening. He showers immediately, no doubt eager to escape his work shirt, trousers and tie. Felix knows the feeling. As Michael rejoins him in the kitchen, his hot, damp presence fills the room. A towel finds his wet mane of hair.

"How is Coleson?"

"Besides being a bastard? He's fine."

Finding a bottle opener in a drawer, Felix uncaps two of the beers. The bottles hiss drily in his hands. "I mean with me taking the week off work."

"He hasn't mentioned it since I spoke to him on Monday. I doubt he's noticed, to be honest."

"Charming."

"It's not as though you're always taking time off. All things considered, you're a model employee. I wouldn't give it another thought."

They finish their first beers, then their second. Slowly a stash of empties begins to grow; brown bottles standing like stems of glassy fungus in the light. They seem out of place in the otherwise clean kitchen; a wet intrusion on the sterile surroundings.

"How are things going with Helen?"

"They're all right." Michael's head vanishes beneath the towel again, emerging moments later vaguely drier. "She didn't take well to me cancelling tonight."

"You had plans?"

"Nothing that couldn't wait."

"You could have seen her, I wouldn't have minded."

"I know you wouldn't have. That's why I didn't mention it."

Michael tells him about all the time Helen and he have been spending together; the evenings out, dinner in the city, sleepy Sundays drifting through the New Forest. None of it sounds especially exciting to Felix, but he can't ignore the discomfort in his stomach, of movement inside him; an unborn chick, still fresh and foetal, yet to break free but stirring now inside its sticky yolk –

"I'm happy for you," he says, and he realises he means it. Not since Rachel broke up with him has Michael spoken at such length about one of his girlfriends. He remembers what Michael said about feeling lost, stripped bare and abandoned, and hopes that he is feeling better now; that Helen has made a difference.

"Enough festering," says Michael, tapping his empty bottle against the work surface and springing suddenly from his seat. "It's Friday night and we have places to be."

"We're going out?"

"We certainly are. Maggie's having a house party and I've RSVP'd for the both of us."

"Maggie?"

"Your work colleague? I realise she must be a distant memory after almost a week off, but she still remembers you."

Felix showers and changes while Michael calls for a taxi. He is still getting dressed when their lift arrives. Sliding onto the back seat of the taxi, he buttons up the top of his shirt while the car pulls away. City lights flash past, catching his face in the reflection of the car window, and he realises his pulse is racing.

Beside him, Michael's face is lit-up. Black skinny jeans cling to his slender legs, a white shirt draining his already pale skin. Michael holds his gaze for a moment. Then he turns back to his window, and Felix does likewise. Taking a deep breath, he closes his eyes, clears his mind and surrenders to the approaching night.

He hears Maggie's house before he sees it, beating with music, nestled noisily in the street. Some effort has been made to black out the windows, bin liners stuck fast to the glass panes, but flickers of strobe light still escape at the edges, shining on tall grass and the children's toys nestled within; plastic tractors and oven sets still speckled with rainfall. There is a potting shed that does not look as though it has seen use in twenty years, flower beds filled with a mixture of daffodils and weeds, and at the front door a thin woman in a large shirt and white skin-tight jeans. She sucks on a cigarette while the door frame supports her, and it is not difficult to associate the sounds of the gulls with her own lips as they pucker and twitch, milking the rollie for every ounce.

Excusing himself, Michael slips past her, and inside. Hurrying after, Felix follows suit.

He has never been to Maggie's house before, and does not think he would recognise it again, were he ever to return here. The hallway is heaving, and he struggles through the press of bodies to keep pace with Michael. On their right, a spare room is being used for storage, a pile of coats and leather jackets like a puddle across the single bed.

They move into the sitting room, made into a rave den, then the basement, where bowls of crisps and dip are doing the rounds. The room is a strange hybrid of home and dance club; wash baskets have been filled with bottles, spotlights stuck on top of dusty utilities. At the far end of the room, a washing machine works its way through a colour wash, filled with orange glow sticks like dancing flames. Everywhere, people are moving to the music's beat.

Faces flock around them, more orange, then green, and white under the wild spotlights, but none of them Maggie's.

"Drinks," Michael mouths, or at least Felix fancies that he does. They each knock back a beer, then another, until they find themselves beginning to dance, helpless not to in this place where private residence meets underground club. Hands find Felix's waist, Michael's face in his face, so close he can see the whites of his teeth, smell the crisp lager on his breath.

They drink more, and dance harder, while their basement surroundings melt slowly away. Behind Michael's head, the washing machine begins a new cycle. Its drum flashes with glow sticks, steadily at first, then faster and faster until the glass door is a blaze of green, burning everything else from Felix's eyes, leaving only spiraling incandescence, Michael's laughing face, then the dark.

A kaleidoscope of chart music fills Felix's ears. People press into him as they squeeze past; hands grasping, firm where they fumble down his wrist. He knows he is at a house party, although he is not sure quite how he got here, or when. His head is a splash of colour and confusion.

Tearing himself from his place on the wall, he wanders through the house. Partly he is anxious, and does not want to draw attention to himself. Mostly he cannot move for other bodies in the way. The kitchen, when he finds it, is a bright, stinking place, alive with hot breaths and the aroma of liquor. Grinning faces hover all around him. He searches for Michael's.

"Down in one," somebody shouts; a tall, bald man with tattoos down his neck.

"Same time next week," chirps a woman beside him, her eyes wide, lush lips smiling.

"Glass is empty –"

"In no hurry –"

"What's a guy got to do to get a drink around here?"

Pushing through the crowds into the next room, he heads further into the house. Another corridor stretches ahead of him, busy and boisterous as the last. Forcing his way between warm bodies, he takes the first opening – a sliding glass door – and finds himself in a kind of conservatory. The music is quieter here, or at least muffled, if not by the glass then the smoke that seems to swell and press against it; mist billowing from cigarettes like rich fumes from exhaust pipes.

"Michael?"

"Who are you?" says a slurred voice. Figures form in the smoke; few and phantasmal.

"Who is anyone? Does it really matter, here?"

"Have you seen Michael?"

"Who the hell is Michael?"

He lingers in the conservatory, surrounded by the semi-formed shapes of the loungers. He cannot help but linger, in this room where there is no up or down, no left or right, no solid forms or certain things, only insubstantial smoke and half-seen shadows shifting in the gloom. For a moment he feels respite from the music, the raucous colours that seem to saturate the rest of the house. Then the shapes of the loungers grow more certain around him.

There is no mistaking the shabby wings, like old bin-liners in the wind, pointed faces with black beaks below which dangle wattles, scarlet like open wounds. Laughter caws from the throats of the assembled, quietly at first then louder; moronic sounds from rough mouths thick with tar, and suddenly there is no safety in the smoke, no sanctuary from the rest of the house or the music, which seems to hammer at his head, slide under his flesh, reverberate his bones and there inside disturb something, which has long waited to be hatched.

He stumbles back from the conservatory. Retracing his steps, he flees through the corridor, the kitchen and the hallway until he reaches the front door, where he does not hesitate but flings it open, throwing himself outside.

"You're leaving?" someone says. The door slams shut behind him.

Quiet settles over him, muting the music from the house. The difference is sobering, as though he has stepped willingly into an ice bath, or the arms of the sea. Cold stings his skin; refreshing, reviving, the most real thing he has experienced all night. Embracing the chill, he begins to walk.

There is a house number, a street name, a city district on a sign beside an abandoned church. Cars line each side of the road, the vehicles perfectly parked. Street lamps illuminate the pavement every few metres or so. Otherwise it is empty; one street in a city made of many. Something that he learned to recognise long ago as loneliness clutches at him, and he looks back to the house, but already it seems dimmer, the music darker, the lights a distant murmur in the night.

A taxi turns into the road, approaching from his left. Its wheels hiss through the gutter as it passes him. When the car draws level, he sees a face staring back from the passenger seat, pressed close to the window; drawn and angular in the dark. He thinks he recognises the face, although he cannot say from where or when. Then the shadows seem to rise up from the gutter and he is afforded one last look at the street, the rooftops, the destitute stars in the night sky, before blackness claims him.

He slips from sleep into vague consciousness, roused by the birds outside the window. As his eyes adjust to the darkness, he recognises the sofa beneath his head, the flat-screen television in the corner, the shape of the sitting room, where he has lived now for a week, and it is a moment before he realises he is back at Michael's house. Distorted by sleep, his surroundings seem strange to him. The man's coat cuts a long silhouette where it hangs in the hallway, a deeper blackness inside the moonlit house.

Rising, he staggers into the kitchen. The tap whines, sending shivers through the piping. He sips a glass of water, relishing the coldness as it slides down his throat. Around him, chrome cabinets shine in the darkness, reflecting even the smallest glimmers of light. Vague memories percolate his mind; a house party, the city submerged, Michael and a taxi. Standing at the sink, he takes another sip.

Outside, the street is stagnant, Miserly Road trapped in the throes of night. And it is still night, he realises. It must be very early. Retreating from the kitchen, he finds his way back to the sofa, and with the smooth leather cushion against his face wonders when this nightmare will end.

The evening comes back to him, then the church, the bar, his office and the long streets that link all these things; the city filled with dark shapes, flapping for flapping's sake, screaming into the sky, desperate to move, to live, to make themselves heard, a blackness in the corners of his eyes and in his ears.

Not for the first time, he wonders why his dreams have resurfaced now. Even Dr. Moore seemed only capable of repressing them. The dejected figure on the church floor fills his thoughts, and with it the vicar's voice, distorted by the imagined heights of the service hall.

"What do they want?"

"To be loved. And to return that love in kind."

He thinks of lovebirds, and wonders why they are called such. Do they love? Are they more than birds because of it, or indifferent except in name? What of scared birds too, and dead birds, and whatdoesitallmeanbirds?

The chirping that woke him grows louder, and it occurs to him that it is not coming from outside. There were no birds visible from the kitchen window, and none that could sing through double glazing. Despite himself, he begins shivering. Almost without realising, his eyes slide back to the indistinct coat, hanging in the hallway.

Time seems to slow as its silhouette shifts. Two tattered arms unfurl from its chest, and it occurs to Felix that it is starving. He does not know for how long it has been standing in the hallway, or what it will take for it to leave.

With its arms outstretched, it turns to face him from the doorway. Though he cannot properly make out its features, he is reminded of the statues from the churchyard, the night after the flood, their smiling faces black with soil and slime. It hovers uncertainly on the threshold of the sitting room, and he can't be sure whether the clicking sound is coming from its throat or the joints in its arms. He imagines that it says a name. Then in one fluid motion it withdraws deeper into the house.

He remains frozen, unable to breathe, as though an ocean of water is pressing down on him. It holds his lips together, threatening to rush into his lungs and drown him from the world once and for all. Silence settles back over the room.

Then he gasps, drawing desperate breaths, struggling from the sofa as though capsized.

"No," he chokes. Like a man asleep, he stumbles through the house. "Not Michael."

His feet carry him to the hallway, then the stairs above. Steps creak beneath his weight, belying the real age of the house, and he is reminded of old flotsam, too long in the water, grown green and riddled with rot. Crossing the landing, he comes to a stop outside a door. The bird sounds are shrill now, almost reptilian in pitch, and he imagines hungry chicks, mouths wide, desperate to be filled. He pushes open the door.

Darkness fills the bedroom, except for the light from the street lamp outside, which floods through the open window. His eyes rush madly around the room, as though seeing it for the first time, but it is the sight on the bed that makes him buckle and cry out, because mounted atop Michael, legs clasped around his hips, skin shining with sweat as it rides him into the mattress, is the figure from his dreams, except this time there is no beak, no marble eyes, no loose dewlaps; just his own face staring back at him, cheeping like a clutch of newborn chicks.

Chapter Eighteen

The sun has not yet risen when Felix slips away from Miserly Road. He quietly packs up what little he brought with him before wandering back into the city. When he reaches the Itchen Bridge, he walks to one side and stares out over the water. Against the vast sprawl of the city, the sea, even the bridge on which he stands, he feels tiny; that speck of silt from so long ago, swirling in the maelstrom. He notices ships in the distance, brooding behemoths barely visible as shadows in the mist. He notices other things, too, which he might have preferred not to see; small slits in the sky, some gliding smoothly, others bobbing as they grow larger, feathered wings beating furiously as they bear down on the bridge.

His flat is as he left it one week ago. In the kitchen he finds a spoon, stained copper with old tea. An empty wine bottle sits on his balcony, filled with black dots; drunk flies and dead flies who did not know when to stop. His covers are still strewn across his bedroom floor from the morning that he left.

Michael rings him several times throughout the day. After letting the first two calls ring off, he sends a reassuring text message. He is fine, after all. There is no need for Michael to worry.

He spends a long time that weekend on the balcony. From where he stands he can see Queen's Park and the docks, the Itchen Bridge, endless buildings rising uniform into the sky, and the sea. Familiar sounds fill his ears; bird cries, long, wilting sounds, and the beating of air beneath wings. Rain soaks him to his skin.

The sea catches his gaze and holds it; a dazzling dance of silvers, greens, blacks, whites and blues. For the first time, he thinks, he does not see grey in the water. It is difficult to believe it is the same sea that swallowed the Titanic over a hundred years ago; the same sea that claimed so many lives that night, glittering now in the shadow of dusk. If it is a testament to man's ingenuity that he can make such ships, that he can keep so much metal afloat, it is a testament to the water that it can take it back at will. The sea is everything in this modern world where people live entire lives as stony statues, never running, flying, loving or singing as they might.

When night falls and he moves inside he can still hear the rain, pattering against his balcony doors. He watches the impact of the droplets as they fall against the glass, and through the curtain of water imagines other things, captured behind; beating wings, bare skin, his face broken apart by the rain –

***

"So, you see, it's your duty to uphold our good name, Felix, as I upheld it when I was a young boy."

Felix and his father were sitting in the Aviary after supper. Outside, evening sank over Crows Hill, bathing the town in shadow. The house had been in his father's family for many generations. Once, a long time ago, it had housed the children who boarded at St. Barnaby's. Felix's father told him that his great, great grandfather had been housemaster in the boarding house's final days. His father told him many things: about living up to expectations, about the history of the town and the importance of their family name.

The cluttered heights of the room towered over him. Photographs lined the mantelpiece, depicting Felix's parents when they were no older than he was now, but it was the birds that would always catch his eyes and hold them. Kestrels, kites, falcons and other kinds he could not begin to name stared glassy-eyed at him from their mounts atop bookcases and on deep shelves. He tried not to look.

"Do you understand the importance? Of fitting in?"

"Yes, I understand. I don't want to be different."

From where he was sitting in his armchair, his father leaned slowly forward. His breath burned with the brandy he kept in a bottle on his desk. "Then don't be. Listen to me, now, because this is important. As men, it's our responsibility to be strong. My father was strong, and his father before him, and when you have a son one day, you'll need to be strong for him, too. Yes?"

Felix couldn't remember having spoken so intimately with his father before. The man's blue eyes burned into his, and in that moment it was impossible to believe he had ever been the young boy from the photographs, smooth-skinned and smiling for the camera. The birds continued to stare down through their hard, artificial eyes from the half-lit heights of their shelves, so much like Harriet's eyes, as they had been afterwards when he found her floating in the churchyard; glazed and empty of whatever had made them bright before.

"I can't help it," he said, more quietly now. "Please, I don't want to be in here."

"Well you must. I don't mean to be hard on you, Felix, but that's the way it is. You'll understand when you're older."

***

In the darkness of his bedroom it is easy to imagine he is back in his father's study. He can still hear the man's voice in his head, smell the brandy on his breath, feel the waxy eyes of the stuffed birds staring down at him from all angles of the room.

When his father went to bed, Felix would pore over the photographs of his parents, searching for something that he recognised. What were his mother and father like, when they were his age? Did they know who they were going to grow up into? His father said that school was Felix's formative years; that it would "make him into the man he would become."

He remembers sitting with Mr. Stuart in an office no less dark or decaying than the rest of the school as he listened to a similar statement. Mr. Stuart said that better schools bred better men; that books birthed intelligence, equipping them with eloquence, with which to take on the adult world.

Were these men better? Felix had wondered, studying his teacher's papery skin, his thin hair and the creases down the lengths of his beige trousers. Like his father, Mr. Stuart had grown up in Crows Hill. Felix had often remarked at the similarities between the two men. Many were the nights he had sat awake in his bedroom, listening to them downstairs talking politics and poetry and the finer details of Odysseus' travels in voices that seemed quite the same. He remembered his father's old checked suits, his reading glasses, his hard eyes like the marbles used to give his stuffed birds sight. And he remembered the Aviary.

It was a horrible name for a horrible room that could not have been further removed from a real bird house. Such places were noisy and bright and alive with the tireless movement of their light-footed occupants. His father's study was a dead room filled with heat, alcohol fumes and fumes with more chemical bite. It was a tomb in which his father locked himself regularly, trodden by the sad ghosts of birds and, Felix had often wondered, perhaps another ghost; his mother, visible to his father in the birds' stale eyes. Felix never knew the truth of this. He knew only that he loved Harriet, and had grown so much already for having done so.

A presence at the foot of his bed draws him back to his room. In his half-asleep state, he imagines a silhouette, skeletal by the window, steeped in city light.

"You're not real."

The base of the bed sinks slightly as it climbs on all fours onto the covers. Hands press their way slowly up the length of the bed, then knees and feet as it moves closer, and with each indentation, each application of weight across his bed, he feels something inside of him, once strange but now almost familiar in the darkness; a heat behind his ribs, beside his stomach, stirring inside his flesh and bone –

Feathered arms drag themselves closer; a swimmer clutching for dry land, or a newborn thing clawing for the first time from embryotic slime. Even when the figure's hands close around Felix's wrists, he does not open his eyes. Its fingers feel hot against his skin. He realises that he is also hot, and hard beneath the covers. A mixture of sweet, rank smells fill his nose, at once maritime and human: sweat and sea and sharp cologne.

"Do you trust me, Felix?" it whispers in a voice that could be his. *"Do you trust me?"*

Hearing himself in the darkness, he stirs. When it does not move from on top of him he struggles, half wrestling with the hands against his wrists. Then he buckles beneath the weight, throwing his body against it. His shouts fill the room as he writhes underneath it until he cannot shout anymore and sinks back into the covers. In this spent state his sleep-filled eyes open.

He knows he is dreaming. He clings to the knowledge, because the alternative is too much to bear. Still, he shouts out at the sight of the face staring back at him; no weeping angel, no beak-mouthed monster, not even his own face, as he had expected, but another; its features sharp, thin eyes locked onto his own.

What little light shines through his window illuminates the face in pools of shadow. Eye sockets seem to extend into the hollows of its skull. Cheeks shine, smooth and unblemished. Long lips stretch into the dark.

"Michael," he says, even though he knows it is not really him. "Michael. Michael."

Then in one fluid motion it leans forward into his face and presses its mouth against his. His body tenses, limbs rigid. When its lips begin to move he slowly softens, leaving only the hardness between his legs, the darkness of the bedroom and the wetness in the corners of his eyes.

Chapter Nineteen

Light floods through the pub windows, revealing rafters and old beams of wood. Dust floats like clouds of sediment on the air, reminding Felix of hulking wrecks, long lost to the bottom of the sea. He finds a table near the back of the room while Michael places an order at the bar. Most of the other Monday patrons are lunching outside, basking in the sun, and there are many tables to choose from.

Michael is not long at the bar. When he returns, he is carrying two cups and saucers. He moves stiffly as he sits opposite Felix and slides one of the saucers towards him. His face is several shades paler than usual, his eyes bruised but bright. They study Felix across the table.

"Coffee," he says, indicating the cup.

"Coffee?"

"Like I used to make. Hopefully better." Reaching out, Michael nudges the saucer closer. "There's sugar. It's hot."

Felix lifts the cup to his lips. As promised, the drink tastes sweet. It reminds him of another time, another life, when Michael made him coffees from the other side of the counter. He takes a second sip.

"Why are we drinking coffee?"

"You look like you could use one. I've ordered food, too."

"You're not exactly the picture of health yourself."

"A sure sign that two men have made the most of their weekend, if you ask me." Michael's smile ghosts across his face. "I found you wandering the streets on Friday night. Care to elaborate?"

"I can't remember."

They sit in silence for several minutes. Felix watches the old man behind the counter as he wipes the sides down. He moves automatically, cleaning the same spot over and over, driving the dishcloth into the wood with what looks like all the force in his knotted arms until Felix suspects he might go through the counter if he carries on.

"You're very quiet," says Michael.

"I'm enjoying my coffee. Thank you."

"Tell me what to do."

"For what?"

"To help."

Looking up, he finds Michael watching him. Even tired, the man appears alert, as though at any moment he might spring from his seat, wings unfurled, and descend on Felix with cutting cheeks, sharp lips and outstretched claws –

"I'm fine, really. I'm still tired from Friday."

"You're a terrible liar. Don't you trust me?"

"Of course."

"So trust me. Talk to me."

Conversation comes unwillingly at first. It is one thing to reflect privately on his past and the events that have helped to shape him. For as long as he has felt separate from everyone else he has been doing just this. But to take these reflections and give them his voice, to make spoken sentences of his memories, seems the most daunting thing. He has never been outspoken. It is much easier to be honest in the dark, where no one will laugh at him, or ignore him, or judge him in any way. Nobody knows him like the dark, or growing dusk, or the shadows inside which he sits, watching and listening but never taking part or being noticed while the rest of the world passes him by.

"This is difficult for me."

"Yes."

"When we say something out loud, that makes it real."

"I think so, yes." Michael's voice slides comfortably into his ears. "As real as anything."

***

Silence filled the dining-room. Outside, evening sank over Crows Hill, bathing the house in cool shadow. The sun hovered at the top of the hill before vanishing behind the treeline. Felix thought he felt it as its light passed the window.

At the head of the table, his father had just finished eating. Cutlery scraped once more against the plate beneath, then clattered quietly where knife and fork were carefully set down.

"How are you finding your sessions with Dr. Moore?"

"They're good. He's good at explaining things." Felix studied his half-empty plate while considering what to say next. "He reminds me of Mr. Stuart."

"Yes, think of him as a teacher." His father nodded approvingly. "And he is helping?"

"What do you mean?"

"Are you still having those dreams?"

"No. I don't think so. If I am, I don't remember them."

He realised his father's hands had been clenched, because they slowly opened as he spoke. In the quiet room Felix heard him swallow.

"You must remember to thank Dr. Moore, when you next see him."

"Does this mean I'm getting better?"

"It does."

"Even though I don't feel better?"

For a long time his father didn't move. Then, rising from his place at the head of the table, he came to stand by Felix. His hand found Felix's shoulder. "We're a family, you and I. There might only be two of us now, but there have been others. Your mother, God rest her soul. Her mother and father, and mine. This is our family. If we have a duty to anything in this life, it's to uphold our family, Felix. Sometimes this means we can't do things we want, or be the people we might otherwise be, but that's the way it is."

"The way what is?"

"Life. The world."

He wanted to tell his father that he knew what he meant. He wanted to be the dutiful son, the normal boy. He wanted to make his father proud. But he couldn't pretend. Catching his eyes, Felix looked quickly away. "I don't understand."

"It's for your own good, Felix. If you understand nothing else, understand that. You'll thank me, one day."

***

Michael leans across the table and for a few moments his hands cup Felix's. His palms are surprisingly soft against Felix's skin, and warm where they've held the cup of coffee.

"How did you cope with that, growing up?"

"I had Harriet. When I was with her I felt better."

"And after Harriet?"

"Dr. Moore. He was the one who suggested I wrote about how I was feeling."

Their food arrives but Felix continues to talk, barely eating, barely noticing the plate sitting before him.

"I can see why you wanted out," says Michael, "and why you haven't been back since. I keep picturing you in the old house, all on your own. No one to talk to. No one to help."

"I thought maybe it was my fault."

"Your fault? What part of anything that you've just told me was your fault?"

"My dreams."

Michael shouts suddenly; a derisive sound that fills the now empty pub. "Christ, Felix, you can't help your dreams. You know that now, right? They're no one's fault."

"But they were bad dreams."

"What were they about? What could possibly have been so bad that it warranted psychiatric care?"

"Nothing."

"Nothing?"

"School," he says quietly, remembering faceless boys with feathered arms, the taste of his own blood in his mouth. "Matthew Petty. The other boys. I remember thinking how much I wanted to be like them, to be their friend, to fit in. They were frightening but I still kept dreaming of them. Dr. Moore called them sea monsters. But he was just trying to help –"

"No, he wasn't. There's one word for what he was doing, and it isn't 'helping'. What do you actually know about him? Who was he?"

"I don't know. He ran a private clinic from his house. He was my father's friend. And he wasn't from Crows Hill. I remember that. Somewhere off the coast, I think. He talked often of the sea."

"Well, the man needs striking off, assuming he hasn't fled back to whichever rock pool he crawled from. And don't get me started on your old man, manipulating you like that. Every boy dreams of monsters. I still do!"

"You do?"

"Yes! It's normal to be frightened, to see shapes in the dark, to fall asleep and think you're flying or drowning. It's our way of making sense of the world, our way of staying sane, day after day. You don't set a psychiatrist on your son, for that!"

"I felt different. From the other boys. I still do."

"Different is good. Celebrate different. Take different's hand and dance with him through the night."

They pick at some limp chips from their plates. The food is cold, and they realise with a start that they have wildly overshot their lunch break. They order more coffee anyway and stay until their plates are clean, the shadows long, their cups drained to the dregs.

Chapter Twenty

When Felix leaves work that evening the city seems subtly changed; an urban place in the beginnings of bloom. Blossom settles in the gutters and across the pavement; pink icing petals on the black road.

People drift like lost souls down London Road. His feet lead him down East Street, past the Engineers' Memorial. In one way, at least, he feels indebted to the statue. Had she not listened to him, he might have drowned in Southampton; the halfway city between the sea and the sky. So many have drowned already. It is not a slight against the city, but the way of men and women, who seem so willing to forget themselves and what it means to be alive.

He is standing in the alcohol aisle of his local convenience shop when his phone rings. Michael had still been talking with Coleson when Felix left the office. Broken from his reverie before the shelves of dark green bottles, he retrieves his mobile from his pocket. "You took your time."

"Can I come over?"

"I thought you were seeing Helen tonight?"

"I need a drink."

"What are we celebrating?"

"My new-found unemployment."

"What?"

"I'll see you in ten, then."

Four bottles of wine find their way into his basket. He navigates the aisles thoughtlessly, hands moving of their own accord between his basket and the shelves. His mind roars with dull white-ocean-noise.

The man behind the till is called Piotr. He has served

Felix many times before. His lips break into a broad smile while he processes the items from Felix's basket, fingers prodding the till screen, but he does not speak. Felix realises he has never heard him speak before, and he finds himself wondering whether he is happy in his work, his life, and whether he too is haunted when he goes to bed at night. Michael's earlier admission to nightmares comes back to him, and Felix suspects he is not alone; that they all dream from the imagined safety of their beds.

Outside the shop, he steps into the coldness of dusk. Shadows drape across the street, and for a moment it is all he can do to stand there while the breath of the city washes over him. Behind him, dust coats the shop window in a thick layer, through which old promotions struggle to surface. Other things, it seems, are also struggling to take form in the dirt; the reflections of the city, swimming like lost shapes beneath brown water. His own reflection swims facelessly among them.

At his flat, Felix has time to roll up his sleeves, remove his tie and pour two drinks before Michael arrives. The door is unlocked and Michael walks straight in. Just before he reaches the kitchen he pauses. Felix cannot see him but he hears that he has stopped in the hallway. Then Michael swoops in and takes up a glass.

"Well," he says. "That's that."

"Are you okay?"

Michael pours the wine down his throat. A thin stream of it escapes his lips, trickling down his chin, almost unnoticeable except where it catches the light. Grey spots grow on the collar of his shirt.

"I'm fine." He coughs to clear his throat, then pours himself a second. "I'm fine. To new beginnings!"

They make an uncertain toast before taking their

glasses to the balcony. The sun is long lost to this side of the building, concealed behind the flats above. This close to the sea, the evening air is quite cold. Hairs prickle down the backs of Michael's arms. Felix realises his own are the same.

"I can't believe it," he says, retrieving a chair from the main room so that he can sit opposite Michael. "After five years of working for him."

"Five years of being late. Five years of lip. Five years of general inadequacy."

"You weren't inadequate."

"It turns out I was quite inadequate. He showed me a chart, with a graph."

The sea breeze struggles against their faces. Felix feels it, like fingers through his hair. Michael's hair remains unmoving, pulled tight into its usual knot, but he sees the breeze in his friend's face; his jaw set, fine nostrils flaring, eyes glistening from the wind and perhaps from something else.

"We could appeal. They can't sack people, just like that. We can fight this."

"Why?"

"What?"

"It's time to move on," says Michael. "It's time for a fresh start."

It might be the sudden breeze, dancing coolly across Felix's skin, or the deep scent of Michael's cologne in Felix's nose, but he cannot still the shiver that runs through him. His wine glass finds his mouth and stays there for several seconds.

"This was always on the cards," adds Michael. "I couldn't have spent my life there any more than you could. It was just a case of when. Well, now I know."

"I'm sorry," says Felix, although he is not quite sure why. "If we hadn't been talking for so long…"

"Don't even think about apologising. That conversation was important. This is good. This is what I need."

They watch the birds that hover in the sky, following their swoops and dives while listening to the drawn-out cries. Even in the shade, beside the sprawling docks and grey concrete piers, the seafront is beautiful. A deep red bleeds into the skyline, and Felix is reminded of the childhood dreams in which he tasted the colour as it ran from his nose.

More than once he finds himself watching Michael. If his friend notices, he does not seem to mind. Felix suspects that he is far away in his own thoughts. The red sky bathes his face, so that he almost appears to glow; a man for five minutes incubated by the warmth of the world, which at all other times seeks to drown them in its depths.

They drink until the wine is gone, their smiles long, the moon a pale disc far out to sea. Tower blocks rise uniform in the night sky, emboldened by the lights lining the Itchen Bridge, together illuminating Queen's Park and the docks beyond. Those blocks of flats that remain dark make silhouettes against the cityscape.

"Did you ever call Angela after that date at the museum?"

"No."

"Of course you didn't." Producing a cigarette from a pack in his pocket, Michael proceeds to light up. He strikes a match; it hisses, spits, then wavers and is swallowed by the night. His second attempt is more successful, and he takes a long drag. "It's going to rain soon."

"How can you tell?"

"Clouds," says Michael, indicating the dark algal blooms that have begun to fill the sky, and although Felix can barely see his friend's face, he can hear the bemusement in his voice. "Clouds usually mean rain."

"I was born in the rain. There was a storm, the roads were blocked. That's why my mother died. I don't think my father ever forgave me for that."

The tip of the cigarette flares in the darkness before descending in hand to rest on Felix's knee. Somewhere nearby, a gull croons gently in its roost.

"So what are you going to do tomorrow?"

"I'm not sure," says Michael, returning the cigarette to his mouth. His smoky breath curls up and away. "Sleep would be good. Sometimes I feel as though I haven't slept in years. Properly slept, I mean. The kind where you wake up the next morning and feel rested."

"I know what you mean."

"I'll pop into the office, to collect my things. To you, I bequeath my third-drawer brandy. We could do lunch again."

"I'd like that."

"The brandy, or lunch?"

"Both."

Michael smokes the cigarette into its grave then lights another. Unencumbered by drink and the dark they talk easily, and only when they feel the first drops of rain do they retreat inside. Felix closes the balcony doors behind them while Michael borrows a coat from his bedroom.

"You're not walking back in this, are you?"

"I like walking," says Michael, "and I don't mind rain."

Felix follows his friend to the door. Shadows fill the

corridor. As he steps into the dark, Michael turns back to him.

"No lights?"

"Broken. Do you think you can find your way to the lift?"

"I'll manage somehow. Cheers for tonight. For the wine, and the company."

"Anytime."

Felix steps forward and wraps his arms around Michael. At first, Michael remains quite still. Then he seems to soften. His chin finds Felix's shoulder, their cheeks pressing together; cold and slightly rough where stubble scrapes his skin. His arms meet behind Felix's back. They stand like this for several seconds while Felix's heart flaps like a trapped bird in its ribcage. Without really knowing what he is doing, he half turns towards the face. His mouth presses against the line of Michael's jaw, then the edge of his lips –

Michael steps quickly back into the corridor. For a moment he waits there, half in and out of the dark. It is impossible to read his face in the shadows. Then he turns from the flat and leaves.

"Michael. Michael, wait."

When Michael does not reappear, Felix returns to the main room. For a long time he sits on the old leather sofa bought to emulate those from their Halls of Residence. Then he gets up and walks to the balcony. Opening the glass door, he steps out into the rain. The garden chair is slippery, and wobbles slightly as he climbs onto it. He stands above the balcony railings. Familiar sounds fill his ears; mewing bird cries, and the beating of air beneath wings. Rain soaks him to his bones.

In his pocket, his phone rings. He feels it, vibrating

against his thigh. Removing the phone, he holds it out over the railings, one arm extended, the other by his side for balance. He takes a deep breath and holds it, feeling the wind against the tears down his face. The chair trembles beneath him.

He calls out for Harriet in a way he has not called for her since he was thirteen. The city takes his voice and throws it back at him. He hears the word as though it echoes through water, distorted until it has no meaning.

His phone vibrates again. He clings to it a second longer before opening his hand and allowing it fall. The phone is swallowed by the darkness but he follows it from the light of its screen as it sinks slowly through the night. When it hits the bottom, there is no sound, as he had previously thought. There is no crash, no splintering of plastic, or soul, or any noise that he can hear from so high above.

He feels the figure behind him before he sees it. Despite himself, he begins shivering. Stepping down from the chair he turns back to the main room and the presence that has been haunting him. Though he cannot make it out properly in the darkness, its silhouette is visible in the doorway.

His heart races while everything else is still. They remain like this for some time, staring at each other across the room. The damp smells stronger now, almost rotten in his nostrils, and he wonders if he has not sunk beneath the sea after all; the full moon wavering like a watery sun. The figure's head cocks curiously to one side. Then it lurches towards him.

He recoils from the advancing figure with a shout, fumbling his way onto the balcony. The railings press against his back. Its movements are sporadic, as though it is in pain. As it staggers closer, he scrunches his eyes shut. He dare not look for fear that it has his face again; that they are one and the same, this sad, malformed thing and he. He cries harder.

Wet fingers brush his skin. Still he does not open his eyes. Damp, maritime smells fill his nose as it moves onto the balcony and wraps him in its feathered arms, no stone cold angel but the opposite; imperfect and alive. It cradles him and kisses him and rocks him while he cries, until he sinks from consciousness into sleep.

Chapter Twenty-One

The alarm clock startles him from sleep. Crawling from bed he silences the sound, staggers into the kitchen and boils the kettle. Crumbs scatter across the floor from the bread that he carries to the toaster. His mouth is sticky, sour-tasting, and as he pours the boiling water into a mug the evening comes back to him; drinks on the balcony with Michael, the sight of the sky and the sea beneath spread out before them, the sound of Michael's laughter and the press of his arms around him, Michael's face against his –

Tea overflows the mug, rushing across the work-surface and down the side of the cabinets. It is a moment before he comes back to himself. Sinking to his hands and knees he chases the spill across the linoleum, slowing its spread with kitchen roll. White tissue becomes rank between his hands.

When he has finished cleaning the spill he pours away the remaining tea. He cleans the mug, and the plates and cups that have been left to drown in the sink, then wipes down the sink and taps. The rest of the kitchen follows; the cupboards, the fridge, the crumbs that have fallen out of reach in the gap between the two units and been left to fester.

He moves onto his bedroom next, gathering up his clothes from the floor and dumping them in the wash-basket. The bed linen follows suit, as do his pillowcases. The clothes horse puts up a fight but he breaks its skeletal back, stripping it bare before folding it away in the airing cupboard. He thrusts his ties, work shirts and trousers into bin liners and leaves them by the door.

The main room looks different in the daytime. Furnishings that are featureless silhouettes by dark resume their roles in the sunlight. His bookcase is a bookcase again, his plastic plant unchanged, the empty drinks cabinet revealed like some kind of lost exhibit, gathering dust. The last thing it held was a half-drunk bottle of cheap rum, weeks ago, when he shared more about himself with Michael than with anyone since he was a child. The evening comes back to him, remembered in his blood, his bones, his fragile heart. His chest tightens until he feels like he can't possibly contain himself and will crack.

He spends a long time in the shower, studying himself in the mirror above the wash basin. Although there is no outward sign of change he feels different. The same slender arms move up and down as they scrub his body. The flannel finds its familiar way through the hollows of his ribs, the arc of his collarbone and the dark pits beneath his arms. Mostly he studies his face, drawn back time and again to his severe eyes. He wonders when they became so serious, so similar to how he remembers his father's eyes looking. He rubs them until the skin around is red and raw.

In his wardrobe he finds a checked shirt, smooth and slightly cold against his skin, and a clean pair of jeans. Before leaving his flat he rummages for the landline. The dusty handset emerges from beneath a pile of magazines. The phone call does not take long.

"I won't be in tomorrow. No, I won't be in Thursday either, or Friday. No. Yes, that's right. Nothing to do with Michael. Why? I've had enough. I know. This is my notice. This. Has anyone ever told you you're a bastard?"

He finds himself on a station platform, stepping onto a carriage. It does not take long for him to be free of the platform, and in a matter of minutes he is staring through dirt-smeared windows as the city from which he has barely moved for eight years passes him by; blocks of flats and parking lots replaced by old brick tunnels and grassy embankments, rising alongside his window as though swallowing the train into their folds.

It is easy to sit here while the rest of the world melts away. Trees stretch into fields, which seem stitched together when viewed from the inside of his carriage; a patchwork of greens and browns and crisp golden yellows tacked beneath blue shining skies. The carriage rocks beneath him, lulling him slowly in his seat, while far above cerulean clouds blossom with wind and rain. He only has eyes for their phosphorescence, their purple twilight tinge, and in the time it takes him to reach the next station he is lost in their depths, rolling with them through the sky; a fish caught in their awesome ocean pull.

The train makes several stops. Each time is the same; the slowing of the carriage while, outside, grey grows in his vision; tall tower blocks, industrial parks that do not deserve to be called parks, cars boxed together behind wire fences, and commotion as passengers surge to their feet with their luggage. Around him the train empties then grows full again, quiet then loud, still then alive with flailing arms and dour faces as everyone staggers for the carriage doors. Through all of this he remains sitting at the back and does not move. Instead he dares to wonder what he is doing here, so far away from the sea, from the city that has become his home.

He knows then he is not running away. He cannot escape himself any more than he can escape the thing perching in the empty aisle seat; his last companion in this mad struggle called life. For thirteen years the bird figure has lived on in the depths of his subconscious; the dream-sea that is torrents of nightmares, unspoken desires and human wishes, slowly transforming into the reeking horror that he recognises now. Without turning from the window he reaches across and takes a misshapen hand in his own. He does not let go again until they arrive at their destination.

The train slows, shudders, pulling into the station at Oxford. Figures file awkwardly down the centre aisle as fresh passengers search for seats. He tags along after those departing.

The street outside the station is clogged with cars, cyclists and sets of lights that do not seem to want to change from red. Like Southampton, this city was founded on water. The name inspires images of black-gowned professors and mortar-board hats; creatures of Mr. Stuart's ilk, and his father's. They call it the City of Dreaming Spires. He remembers parks – real parks, with old trees and trimmed lawns – from when he used to visit the city with his father, and punts, floating like swans on the Cherwell, the Bridge of Sighs and All Souls College guarded by curlicue gates and gargoyles, water tumbling from stone mouths locked into snarls. He crosses the road and keeps walking until he finds a bus stop.

It is raining by the time the bus arrives. Clouds weigh heavily over the city. The double-decker draws to a stop alongside the shelter, doors hissing as they draw apart to let him in. As he steps on board a wave of sickness rides him at the thought of where he is heading. He feels as though a cocktail of emotion is curdling inside him; lumps of white upset floating on a thin skin of anger and sharp acid pain. He wonders if he has made the right decision in returning after all these years; if he made a decision at all or whether his feet have guided him here of their own accord. Then he is buying a ticket, finding a seat, and it is too late for doubt and second thoughts.

Chapter Twenty-Two

Silence settled over Crows Hill Church, broken only by the sounds of small birds twitching in the trees and the muffled crunch of twigs beneath Felix and Harriet's school shoes. The air was cold, the soil springy with water and slime. Ancient gravestones guided them through the grounds where it was almost possible to hear the church, ringing with early hymns, to taste the rigours of religion on their tongues; the hallowed heart of Crows Hill, guarded by grey angels and their cherubim children.

"It's so peaceful here," said Harriet, ducking under branches and dragging her hands across the gravestones. "And private. When I come here I feel like I'm the only person in the whole world."

"Now there's two of us," said Felix, following behind her.

She turned as she ducked beneath a low branch, and smiled.

They foraged further through the undergrowth, as though looking for something, though Felix had no idea what that might have been. Sometimes Harriet would stop to study a headstone, running her fingers along the weathered inscriptions. Other times it was the statues that held her attention. Felix followed her lead.

"They love the rain, you know," she said, stopping by one of the statues near the back wall of the church. An old, angelic face stared back at her, its smile lopsided where its features had begun to wear away.

"How can you tell?" said Felix, coming to stand beside her.

"You can see it, in their faces. I think I would love the rain, if I was made of stone. I love the rain anyway." She scooped up a handful of slippery soil. "It's so refreshing."

"I was born in rain," said Felix, almost fumbling over his words in his hurry to speak them. "In that flood, the big one that everyone talks about. The roads were all blocked, so my mother couldn't reach the hospital. She died giving birth to me in her bed, with the rain against the windows. There hasn't been a flood that bad since."

"That's special, you know." Using the base of the angel for support, Harriet sank cross-legged to the ground. "It doesn't sound it, but it is. No one else in the whole town can say that."

"I don't think they'd want to."

"Sometimes I don't think I'm from this town at all." Harriet's fingers sank into the grassy mud and stayed there. "Sometimes when I watch the others at break-time, running and shouting together, I feel like I don't fit in. Then I come here and I feel better. And the statues always play with me in the rain."

Once she had finished talking, Harriet sprang to her feet and danced. She moved dreamily; school dress fluttering, her shoes stepping lightly on the grass, seeming detached from the world as she swayed and span to some secret, silent waltz. The statues stood around her, their sad, smiling faces fixed onto the girl, but Felix had only eyes for Harriet as she celebrated the soil and the sky and the statues around them.

She continued to dance until she lost her balance and tumbled into Felix. They laughed as they both fell over. He knew the wetness of mud against his arms, the damp that soaked into his school clothes from the grass, the silvery sound that was Harriet's happiness, and in that moment the world could have ended for all he cared.

***

He might be in a dream again, standing by the side of the road where he would wait on Saturday mornings while his father queued in line for the post office. It is hard to believe that he is here. He once swore to himself that he would never come back and yet it feels like he might not have left at all; as though all the years in between his leaving and returning have meant nothing, undone in hours. Breathless he begins to walk.

The high street seems shorter, narrower than he remembers. He recognises the butcher's, and the fabric shop, and the old post office that belonged to Mrs. Grantham. A sheet of plywood blocks the door, black with damp. The window above is a dark, empty space.

He is drawn past a supermarket and a new cinema complex. At the end of the street is the town square, where they would hold the market on Wednesdays. There is a coffee shop now and, on one corner of the square, a bar or nightclub, stirring with activity in the fading light. Most of the shops are closed, and few people cross his path. A young boy kicks an empty can across the square, soundless as they stop start down the street. Across the road Felix spies a woman, face deadpan as she clutches a buggy, and moments later a man, grey suit clinging to grey skin, inside which he seems to wriggle, as though sloughing business attire and the false flesh beneath it.

St. Barnaby's is not far; ten more minutes through the town. The school, at least, has not changed. The school gates are rough against his hands, and cold when he presses his face against the old iron bars. With his vision blinkered he could be staring straight into the past; a part of Crows Hill trapped in time behind the old school walls. In the distance, across the playing fields, he can just make out the grounds. Strips of grass have been mowed short, made suitable for the cricket season, dotted with clusters of crows. He remembers floods of footsteps, shouts as boys flocked through the corridors and the shrieks of girls as they flapped noisily after one another on the playing fields. When he steps back from the gates, rust has coloured his palms an orange-red.

A strange relief sinks over him. The feeling is unexpected but welcome. He realises it is not the town itself that comforts him – there is no love lost there – but the sight of some place familiar. In Southampton, people have forgotten, as people are prone to do, the history that has helped define them. He thinks of Old Town, crumbling away out of sight and mind, and the pocket watch in the museum, as broken and beautiful as the city itself. He wonders how much of the city he has really seen, how much of the world he sees and how much slips past him, unnoticed by most, except perhaps those who look, who have nothing else to distract them. He was no different, until the evening at East Park when he stopped and for five minutes listened to the city, reminding him of a face, a girl, a time when he ran in the rain, and slipped in the mud, and laughed until his eyes were as wet as his clothes.

Turning from the school gates, he takes a small footpath and finds himself outside the house that once doubled as Dr. Moore's clinic.

The same Victorian standards that seem to have held the town in their unerring grasp reflect back at him from the front of the building. Detached from the rest of the street, it stands apart. Tall windows stare blindly outwards, the glass opaque with dust, behind which floral-pattern curtains cascade like rotting mulch. The porch is still there, the balconies, the black slate roof that characterises most of the town's properties, but all of it is worn, as though it has not been tended to for many years now. Wood that was white is yellowed and flecked with wear. A small garden thrives with neglect beneath the porch, bushes scratching unchecked against the old wooden posts.

The house is obviously unoccupied, but that does not deter him from lifting the latch on the front gate. Nettles brush his jeans as he walks into the shadow of the house, and he finds himself wondering if it is really neglect that has transformed the building, or whether such rot was inevitable, in this place where dreams lapped like surf so closely to reality and on more than one occasion may have leaked through; Dr. Moore's sea, seeping into the woodwork, licking the paint from the walls, turning the curtains into slick, tumbling weeds.

The front door looms before him. He might reach out, turn the handle, force the sodden wood with his shoulders and find himself in the hallway where he had once stood with his father when he met Dr. Moore for the first time. It would not be difficult. A muffled silence settles over him. He grasps the iron door knocker, once too high for him to reach, and finds it in the shape of a slender octopus.

He wonders if Dr. Moore was ever a psychiatrist or if he only purported to be such, and was in fact something else. His esoteric counselling was most unconventional. Psychiatry should involve medicine; he knows this now. And yet there were never any medicines he can remember taking; no pills, no tablets, nothing except Dr. Moore's teachings, which did not seem strange at the time but appear infinitely so now that they have resurfaced. One of the mantras echoes in his head like the crashing of surf inside a shell.

"When a person sleeps, he floats through this sea and the waves forms shapes around him. The feeling is quite awesome, in the proper sense of the word. There is no escaping the sea, into which we must all fall when we sleep."

Seemingly on a precipice, he hovers outside the door. The suckered arm of the door knocker is cold against his skin and resistant when he lifts it from its place. Rust grows like algae between the joints. When he lowers it back to the door, the sound is soft with damp.

He is not sure what he expected to happen. The silence stretches out, filled only by a faint sigh, which he presumes is the wind through the garden. His weight shifts, the porch groaning underneath him, and for a moment he thinks he sees the curtains shiver, disturbed not by the wind, or human hand, but a different current, running through the rotten fabric like fingers through hair. When they do not move again, he departs, leaving the house behind him; silent like a shipwreck lost to the bottom of the sea.

The dour face of the town yields to darkness and with it the ghosts of a place he finds familiar. He walks until the streets give way to more patchwork fields, where he used to run with Harriet, chasing her through the yellow sheaths of corn, into the next field, and the next, until they collapsed from exhaustion into the crops. The fields are empty now. The tang of fertiliser stings the air.

It is almost dark when he reaches the churchyard. The climb is slippery, the grass still wet from recent rain. He wonders if it was the same rain that fell over Oxford, hours earlier, the same rain that washes in from the sea over the city that has sprung up by the coast. It smells the same in his nose, looks just as wet against the glistening toes of his shoes.

He wanders from the path, treading trails reclaimed by the undergrowth. Weeds fester in the darkness, and grasses, allowed to grow tall unchecked. As he moves deeper into the grounds, figures begin to emerge from the gloom; a glimpsed face, an armless bust, a severed head staring him out from its home in the hollows of a tree. He reminds himself that he has nothing to fear. They are just statues; stone chiselled into shapes that man might better recognise.

The statues have suffered terribly in the years of his absence. Limbless, they regard him with the uncanny sightlessness of sculptures, while others watch from faces with no nose, or mouths that stretch too long from cheek to cheek. Harriet introduced him to them all, once, and their cherubim children; round faces peering up at him from the grass. They were her friends. Everyone needs friends.

His feet pick careful passage through the graves. The headstones are broad, immodest slabs detailing names and dates, furry with moss and white bird-stains. As he makes his way towards a marker, near the church walls, a scratching sound reaches his ears.

Like the school, this quiet corner, at least, seems to have survived. If it is strange that he feels relief at the sight of the school and the church, it is stranger that he should resent the way the town has changed. Had he not felt trapped by the school gates, the town's old, tired ways?

Movement draws his eyes to the dark roof of the church, where something pale is squirming against the slate. When it reaches the end of the roof, he fancies it leans forward; peering down from the guttering. Then it drags itself from the edge, tumbling through the space between the roof and the ground; falling heavily like a chick from its nest.

As it tumbles through the blackness, he is reminded of a cherub, brought to life by the dark and the rain. He doesn't remember ever seeing the cherubim move before, but he still feels a swell of familiarity at the sight of the plummeting shape. Harriet believed. It is not such a stretch of the imagination to think that the angels' children played with Harriet and their stone parents in the rain.

It hits the ground with a soft thump. For a moment it lingers where it has fallen, on the earth beside Harriet's grave. He wonders if it has always waited here; if this is where it once hatched and for a short while at least hopped through the wet grass in the tall shadow of the spire. The feeling of familiarity grows stronger, drawing him towards the solitary shape. He is several feet away when it turns from the grave in his direction.

Cheeks still plump with childhood fill the face, no cherub but his own thirteen-year-old self staring up at him; Felix White as he last was before he lost himself, growing into the thin, misshapen thing that has haunted his waking dreams.

He sees all this in a second stretched by shock and disbelief. Then he falls back from the boy into the grass.

The boy watches him fall. Then he too crumples to his knees. With his face in his small hands, he begins to weep. Felix recognises the quiet sobs from a dozen sleepless nights and wonders how long the boy has been crying. He wonders if he cries every night and if anyone has ever noticed, before now. Something wells up inside him; an irrepressible wave of feeling, pushing at his chest until he thinks he might break, burst open, filling with water and night.

"Some stories show them with the bodies of birds and the faces of women," declares the boy, repeating a lesson committed to memory. "In others, they are depicted as beautiful maidens, with talons for feet and great feathered arms. Some say they devoured the flesh of those who were drawn to them, and that they sang out of hunger. Others portray them as victims of their own voices, for those who were drawn to them could never leave, and so starved to death on their island prisons, which became islands of corpses, carcasses resting amid the meadows and the flowers that grew from them."

The mention of the meadow no longer frightens Felix. He has seen the alternative, lived years in its shadow, and it means nothing. There is so much pain in the world. There is so much hurt. It is a wonder how one man can take it, how he is expected to live, to go on, when nothing is ever fair, or seems to make sense, or matters at the end.

"They love the rain, you know," says the small voice, and Felix's hand moves to his mouth. "You can see it, in their faces. I think I would love the rain, if I was made of stone. I love the rain anyway."

The headstone seems smaller than he remembers. He has grown up since he was last here, and yet there is a part of him that has not grown; not properly, at least. For thirteen years it has lived on, becoming rank and rotten in the depths of his subconscious; the dream-sea that is torrents of nightmares, unspoken desires and human wishes. He breathes heavily.

"I meant to tell you something that night, Harriet. I was scared, but I knew you'd understand. I think that if I'd told you, it would have made it real. It might have helped. But I never got the chance."

He realises he is happy for Harriet, because she was

spared when the Sirens took her to that place which is sea and sky and blackness, filled with burning stars and coral fish and dancing dreams of the rotting dead. His own hands rise to cover his face. When he removes them again, the boy is gone.

He says his goodbyes to Harriet and then he leaves. His feet retrace their steps; past the church, the hill, the fields that once seemed to stretch on forever. The town shines in the night. Light floods from the vast windows of the supermarket and above the nightclub, illuminating a high street alive with shifting silhouettes; the townsfolk awakened by night and the promise of dreams. Around Felix, litter bins overflow with water, gutters flooding with the dark. People step into one another and do not step back, so that the streets through which he walks turn into cloying, clay-like masses shaped by the slick hands of the town, wrung-out like sopping dishcloths, drained of everything except water, from which there is no end.

He stops one more time on his way to the night bus, outside a manor house not far from St. Barnaby's. There is a hedgerow beside the driveway where he waits, watching the well-lit windows for movement. It is a cloudy night, the blackness above seeming to frame the building. Time loses all meaning in the dark.

It is difficult to see anything of the man who eventually draws the curtains. He moves from window to window throughout the house, dousing the lights one room at a time. His progress is slow but steady, and Felix sees a man trapped by ritual; re-enacting the same movements that he made eight years ago, and eight years before that. Even while the town around him has twisted and changed he has not; clinging to the same tired fabric of the curtains each night as he clung to his grief, preserved out of feathers and formaldehyde in the glass cases in the Aviary.

"Are you listening to me? Because this is important. Don't be frightened. As men, it's our responsibility to be strong. My father was strong, and his father before him, and when you have a son one day, you'll need to be strong for him, too."

As a boy, Felix remembers thinking about the man his father had become versus the short, skinny boy in the photographs on their mantelpiece. He wondered if he would grow up to be like William White one day; tall and thin and wise about the world. He could not imagine a life without his father watching over him, teaching him right from wrong. That is what fathers are for, after all. And yet he has managed it.

When the man reaches the dining-room window he pauses, and Felix shivers with panic at the prospect of being seen. He knows that he is too far away from the house, and it is dark, but these rational thoughts do nothing to still his soaring heart. Despite himself he huddles further into the hedgerow.

Then the man draws the dining-room curtains, and the front of the house falls into darkness. When Felix realises he will not see his father again, he turns from the town, as he turned from it once before, and walks away.

Chapter Twenty-Three

The waterfront draws him across Queen's Park, back to the place where he has spent so many happy nights. As he approaches the bar, he is struck by how different it looks in the light. It seems diminished, as though it is the dark, or perhaps the presence of its patrons, that revives the bar each night.

He orders a pint and some lunch from the menu before finding a seat outside. The glass doors are open to the seafront, offering an uninterrupted view of the water. Settling into a chair by the smoking terrace, he relishes the peace and quiet.

If Michael were here, this is where they would be sitting. He would probably be smoking. Felix can picture his friend's cheeks, drawn as he sucks on a cigarette. His hair is tied back from his face, his eyes thin against the wind.

Felix's beer finds his lips. The drink is cold as it slips down his throat. He shivers in his seat but does not stop drinking until half of the pint is gone. Returning his glass to the table, he stares out over the water. The water stretches on, as far as he can see, until there is no sea, no sky, no white-tipped waves, only a distant blur that is all of these things bled together.

By the time his food arrives, his glass is empty. He orders another drink, and another when the waitress comes to take his empty plate. With every pint the sky grows brighter, the sea darker, the bar around him less distinct, until he really could be in an ocean village, sunk far beneath the sea. Birds hover in the sky and he fancies they are Sirens, sprung from the depths to haunt him with their cries.

Felix does not know what came over him the other

night, standing in the corridor outside his flat with Michael, except that it felt right. He is not sorry for what happened. He is only sorry that it has taken him this long to realise who he is and what matters.

***

"Three died that night. One of them a child, as well. Swept clean away by the waters."

"Clean? I saw one go myself," said Mrs. Grantham, "and there was nothing clean about it."

"You saw one?"

"With my own eyes," she said. "Susan Stark. Thrashing in the cold and the wet, clothes soaked through, kicking her arms and legs right until she rounded the street and I lost sight of her. I tell you, there was nothing clean about it, or the remains."

"Goodness. The remains?"

Mrs. Grantham shook her head and dabbed a small handkerchief to her mouth before speaking. "They found her in the school grounds, all limp and bruised. Then there was Jake, one of the Wilsons, though they've since moved away, bless them. And the Green's young girl, face like a little cherub. Friends with that queer one, William White's son. Terrible business, that winter. Cars, lifted straight down the roads. And the statues, from the churchyard! I don't think I'll ever quite forget it."

When they had finished speaking, Felix fled the sounds of their voices. He ran as far as the church, where he scrabbled over the old stone wall and hid among the headstones. His face burned, his sweat cold, his chest tight as though he was floundering amid the flood waters and every breath was a struggle for air. The enormity of that night washed over him; the village upheaved, the very angels that now watched over him swept on stony wings into the streets, and more than anything else the realisation that he was alone again, with only a dream of bird-shaped boys for company.

***

Evening falls, then night, the waterfront lighting up, illuminated by the various other bars and restaurants beside it. He drinks until the bar blurs behind his eyes. Slowly the smoking terrace fills with people, the sort who cannot wait for Friday, come to escape their homes, the streets, the city for a night. Content, he sits among them.

Laughter fills his ears, seeming to carry across the sea. The sound belongs to three men, sitting across the terrace. As he finishes his beer, he wishes he could laugh as they are laughing. Instead he imagines Michael sitting beside him, spouting his typically blasé philosophies.

Staring around, he realises he is the only one sitting by himself. If anyone is concerned for him, they do not show it. He might be Sam, forgotten by everyone except a statue; the angel who alone loves the city and the people who call it their home. He thinks about love and what it might feel like. He thinks about death and when it was that they all died. He thinks about the plant in the corner of his flat with its plastic fronds, its sterile soil, its bright, synthetic stem, until it is all he can do not to close his eyes, ball his fists and scream at the top of his voice.

The men's laughter begins again, rising uproariously across the terrace. Their eyes are creased, their white teeth gleaming, throats hollow holes as they laugh beneath the stars. In that moment they could all be Sirens; every man and woman with blood in their veins and a hunger for singing, for screaming, for dancing through the iridescent night, and the grey days that follow.

The buffeting of bird wings catches his attention. On the railings beside the waterfront a solitary gull struggles to maintain its balance. He does not look at anyone for a long time, instead staring out across the water. The gull is a small, pale shape against the vast blackness of the sea behind it, except not solely black but white and silvery, even gold where the light from the waterfront ignites the sharp tips of the waves, and all of it shivering beneath the moon.

"It's beautiful, isn't it?"

It is a moment before Felix realises the voice is real, and not imagined. Turning, he looks up at the man standing beside him at the table. Michael does not look back but continues to stare out to sea.

"Michael?"

With his head down, Michael laughs quietly. His breath is heavy with beer. Felix wonders what is so funny, before realising that he is mistaken in the darkness.

"Michael? What's wrong?"

Reaching across, Felix grasps his friend by the wrist. His fingers feel the sleek black jacket, the wrist bone beneath; hard from walking, from shaking. Here is a man laid bare, brought low by liquor and life. When Felix next speaks, the waves almost swallow his words.

"What's happened?"

Michael's head turns slowly. Glazed but honest eyes stare back at Felix. His silhouette trembles before the interior light of the bar. "I'm wildly unhappy."

The sea draws a cold, silent breath and seems to hold it.

Michael lurches, stumbling into him. Felix sinks back into his chair, his head spinning as a quick mouth finds his. Shadows scatter like a flock of frightened birds around him.

He allows Michael the kiss. He needs it just as much; to feel the drink-lacquered lips against his own. Michael's hand grasps his wrist, gentle at first, then suddenly tight, and under the warmth of his mouth and the grip of the hand Felix finally cracks. His heart races as he imagines something long-repressed pecking through his ribs and intercostal flesh, hatching from his hurried chest, rearing its fresh, amniotic face in the darkness –

"You were right," Felix says, too quietly for anyone to hear except the man whose mouth hovers by his own. "I was right. This is what it's all about."

Light melts around them, and shadows, flapping in the glass terrace doors; silhouettes and reflections free to celebrate alongside the bodies that cast them. Inside, people bounce to the beat of the music, arms thrown in the air; plumage lank like those of seabirds washed up in oil. Others hold each other tightly, tattered wings linking shoulders, waists and withered chests, while beaked mouths stretch into grins. Still they dance because there is nothing else to do, no horror greater than that which they find themselves in; not the feathered bone-arms but the broken world, a decaying hull in which they are all trapped, except for these brief moments, glimmering like slimy pearls in the darkness.

Michael's mouth pauses, breaks away. His face glows by the bar light, and Felix realises it is easier here, that it would always have happened in this place where they come, not to lose themselves, but to find themselves by the roar of the sea. He is part of that sound, a speck of silt in Southampton's muddy waters. They are all specks; swirling, sinking, rising in the sparkling oblivion of the depths. With the realisation comes laughter, bubbling up from inside him.

Sparkling Books

We publish:

Crime, mystery, thriller, suspense, horror and romance

YA fiction

Non-fiction

All titles are also available as e-books from your e-book retailer.

For current list of titles visit: *www.sparklingbooks.com*

@SparklingBooks